# A Candlelight Estasy Romance

**"DON'T PULL THE HAUGHTY ICE QUEEN ROUTINE WITH ME, LADY. IF WE WERE IN A NORMAL SITUATION, I'D KISS YOU SENSELESS."**

"What makes you think I'd ever let you near me if we were in a normal situation?" she spit at him, her blue eyes raking over his muscular body. "Don't overestimate yourself. I don't need you or any other man."

Step by step Mike closed the gap between them. "For a doctor, you don't know much about biology. It's time you learned that making love isn't a mental exercise."

"Making love? I have no intention of—"

"Neither did I until now," Mike said ominously.

## CANDLELIGHT ECSTASY ROMANCES®

258 PROMISE OF SPRING, *Jean Hager*
259 TENDER AWAKENING, *Alison Tyler*
260 DESPERATE YEARNING, *Dallas Hamlin*
261 GIVE AND TAKE, *Sheila Paulos*
262 AN UNFORGETTABLE CARESS, *Donna Kimel Vitek*
263 TOMORROW WILL COME, *Megan Lane*
264 RUN TO RAPTURE, *Margot Prince*
265 LOVE'S SECRET GARDEN, *Nona Gamel*
266 WINNER TAKES ALL, *Cathie Linz*
267 A WINNING COMBINATION, *Lori Copeland*
268 A COMPROMISING PASSION, *Nell Kincaid*
269 TAKE MY HAND, *Anna Hudson*
270 HIGH STAKES, *Eleanor Woods*
271 SERENA'S MAGIC, *Heather Graham*
272 A DARING ALLIANCE, *Alison Tyler*
273 SCATTERED ROSES, *Jo Calloway*
274 WITH ALL MY HEART, *Emma Bennett*
275 JUST CALL MY NAME, *Dorothy Ann Bernard*
276 THE PERFECT AFFAIR, *Lynn Patrick*
277 ONE IN A MILLION, *Joan Grove*
278 HAPPILY EVER AFTER, *Barbara Andrews*
279 SINNER AND SAINT, *Prudence Martin*
280 RIVER RAPTURE, *Patricia Markham*
281 MATCH MADE IN HEAVEN, *Malissa Carroll*
282 TO REMEMBER LOVE, *Jo Calloway*
283 EVER A SONG, *Karen Whittenburg*
284 CASANOVA'S MASTER, *Anne Silverlock*
285 PASSIONATE ULTIMATUM, *Emma Bennett*
286 A PRIZE CATCH, *Anna Hudson*
287 LOVE NOT THE ENEMY, *Sara Jennings*
288 SUMMER FLING, *Natalie Stone*
289 AMBER PERSUASION, *Linda Vail*
290 BALANCE OF POWER, *Shirley Hart*
291 BEGINNER'S LUCK, *Alexis Hill Jordan*
292 LIVE TOGETHER AS STRANGERS, *Megan Lane*
293 AND ONE MAKES FIVE, *Kit Daley*
294 RAINBOW'S END, *Lori Copeland*
295 LOVE'S DAWNING, *Tate McKenna*
296 SOUTHERN COMFORT, *Carla Neggers*
297 FORGOTTEN DREAMS, *Eleanor Woods*

# FIRE AND ICE

*Anna Hudson*

*A CANDLELIGHT ECSTASY ROMANCE®*

Published by
Dell Publishing Co., Inc.
1 Dag Hammarskjold Plaza
New York, New York 10017

Copyright © 1985 by Jo Ann Algermissen

All rights reserved. No part of this book may be reproduced or transmitted in any form or by any means, electronic or mechanical, including photocopying, recording or by any information storage and retrieval system, without the written permission of the Publisher, except where permitted by law.

Dell ® TM 681510, Dell Publishing Co., Inc.
Candlelight Ecstasy Romance®, 1,203,540, is a registered trademark of Dell Publishing Co., Inc., New York, New York.

ISBN: 0-440-12690-8

Printed in the United States of America
First printing—January 1985

*To Dr. E. K. Gibson, neighbor, friend, NASA scientist who has been to the Amundsen-Scott Antarctic station. Many thanks for sparking my imagination and providing materials to make this fictitious novel have a realistic flavor.*

*Also to the National Science Foundation, Division of Polar Programs, for the pictures, research programs, and manuals.*

To Our Readers:

We have been delighted with your enthusiastic response to Candlelight Ecstasy Romances®, and we thank you for the interest you have shown in this exciting series.

In the upcoming months we will continue to present the distinctive, sensuous love stories you have come to expect only from Ecstasy. We look forward to bringing you many more books from your favorite authors and also the very finest work from new authors of contemporary romantic fiction.

As always, we are striving to present the unique, absorbing love stories that you enjoy most—books that are more than ordinary romance. Your suggestions and comments are always welcome. Please write to us at the address below.

Sincerely,

The Editors
Candlelight Romances
1 Dag Hammarskjold Plaza
New York, New York 10017

## *CHAPTER ONE*

"Get that compressor fixed or we're all going to freeze," Dr. Kelle Langdon bit out into the dry frozen air inside the geodesic dome at the Amundsen-Scott South Pole Station.

"Damn," Mike Johnson cursed when the bolt he'd been trying to get into position slipped between his mittens for the third time and dropped into the packed snow. "Lady, have you ever tried to screw something on with the equivalent of three pairs of mittens on your hands? Nobody is going to freeze. If worse comes to worst, and it won't, we'll drag out the emergency heaters."

When she heard his words, twin dangers crossed Kelle's mind: fire and carbon monoxide. In the desert land of ice the danger of fire was always in the minds of each of the twenty wintering scientists and support personnel. Ice had to be melted and purified for their drinking water; there would never be enough water to extinguish a fire. And carbon monoxide poisoning was particularly dangerous because it was often not apparent right away.

As she glanced down at the hunched figure in front of her, a look of alarm spread over her face. She'd been thinking about the possibility of fire when the white signs of frostbite painted themselves above the dark full beard on Mike's cheeks. Without hesitation she planted her feet on either side of his red parka, curved her body over his, placed her mittened hands over the affected area, and spoke softly. "Exhale slowly. Frostbite."

"I'll get it on this time," he promised. The warmth of his breath changed to miniature puffs of crystallized ice. The slow wink he shot Kelle made her shiver, not from the cold, but from fear of the unknown.

For six and a half months Kelle and the others had been virtually stranded in the icy wasteland conducting various types of scientific research, much of which would benefit the space program. But for the first time, she was frightened. Of what? she questioned. No heat? Her chin rubbed against the thick pile of the inside of her hood as she shook her head. With precautions they could minimize the possibility of fire. But what could be done to minimize the fire making my fingers tingle right now? she wondered, lightly touching the trimmed edge of Mike's beard with her thumbs. I bet I'd be feeling the cold by now if it was anyone else's face beneath my hands, she thought ruefully.

Silently Kelle chuckled. The long polar months must finally be taking their toll on her libido. The smile curving her lips widened. How would she be able to explain caressing a fellow participant in the wintering-over expedition when she had so firmly and persistently rebuffed the advances of the other men on the expedition, men who had naturally been interested in the only woman at the Pole?

Celibacy isn't any more difficult for men than it is for women, she silently told herself. And Mike Johnson would tempt any woman, any place, any time. Tall, powerfully built, he was a man few woman could ignore.

"How's it going?" Kelle asked, determined to change her pattern of thought.

For a split second, Mike raised up, pressing his back against her. Her own weight from shoulder to thigh momentarily touched the curvature of his back. "Fine. Better," he answered.

Why better? she wanted to ask, but didn't.

Something prevented her from bantering with him as she did with the other members of the team. She realized for the first time that she seldom spoke to Mike. She watched him covertly but seldom engaged in conversation with him. Strange, she realized, when she considered herself an equal, a buddy to the other men. Was the reason behind her reticent behavior an instinctive fear that he could light the fires she had protectively banked before making the journey to the South Pole?

Mike shifted his weight to the right, reaching for a wrench. Through the double thickness of their parkas Kelle felt, or imagined she felt, his supple back muscles stretch, then contract. A flush colored her face as she felt the tips of her breasts harden in response.

"I've got it," Mike whispered aloud. "Just a moment longer and I'll have it working again."

Little do you realize what else you have working, she thought wryly. Quickly she dismissed the idea. As medical doctor for the winter polar expedition, she rationalized, she would have administered the same first aid to anyone in danger of frostbite.

Kelle straightened. Assuming her professional voice, she instructed, "Johnson, check in at the infirmary when you've finished."

"Wait a minute. . . ." Mike jumped to his feet.

Kelle could feel the tension between them. It seemed to hang in the air drawing them closer together. She turned away quickly, severing the ties threatening to bind them.

She didn't answer when she heard his low voice calling her name through the frigid air. Ignoring the urge to turn, Kelle stomped the loose snow off her mukluks before entering the double wooden doors of the hut.

But she did ask herself the question: Why now? Why had he called her Kelle instead of the casual Doc or lady? Something eerie had happened under the aluminum dome. She didn't understand what or how . . . or why. But something was responsible for her increased heart rate and the dizzy sensation she experienced. Stop it, she ordered herself. You're making an iceberg out of a snowball.

Petersen, Schwartz, and Kleinschmidt raised their heads simultaneously as Kelle entered the room.

"Mike take care of the heating problem?" Carroll Kleinschmidt questioned as he rose to his feet and advanced toward Kelle.

"He has everything under control," she said, removing her mittens and parka before bending down to take off her mukluks.

"How about a cup of coffee? You look frozen," Carroll offered.

Kelle's stomach churned. "Sounds good."

Glancing toward Jon Petersen and James Schwartz, she asked, "Anything new on the seismology reports?"

They'd received a message earlier in the day, via a ham operator, that St. Helens volcano in Washington State was on the verge of erupting. The three men had been poring over seismology reports ever since.

"Nothing significant," James muttered. "We may need your help later."

Straightening, Kelle nodded. Support personnel often assisted the scientists by taking readings on the various mechanical devices. "If Mike isn't inside in ten minutes call me. I'll drag him back in here if necessary!"

Following Carroll out of the work area, through the walkway, into the lounge area, Kelle rubbed her hands and blew on them.

"You taking some vitamin pill you aren't giving the rest of us?" Carroll teased, grinning.

Kelle watched his retreating back, sat down at the table, and removed her thick-lensed glasses from the front pocket of her plaid wool shirt. "No. Why?"

Blue eyes twinkling he laughed aloud. "I figured if you thought you had the strength to haul the local Paul Bunyan back in here, you must be holding out on us."

Chuckling, Kelle put two spoonfuls of sugar into her steaming mug. Sugar is good for shock, she thought, trying to still her thudding heart. "I'm a big girl, but I guess I'm not quite that strong," she admitted. The heat from the cup fogged her still-cold glasses.

"Oh, I don't know. There are times when I think Elizabeth drags me around by my nose."

His mentioning his wife's name gave Kelle the excuse she needed to get the topic of conversation away from Mike Johnson. "What's the latest?"

"The boys are fine. She's fat and pregnant."

"Dr. Kleinschmidt—pregnant ladies aren't fat," she rebuked him playfully.

"Oh, no? You should have seen her when she was pregnant with the twins." His arms circled in front of him as he leaned back on two legs of his straight-back chair. "Humongous!"

Kelle chuckled as she chastised, "Some way for a proud papa to talk."

"Young Carroll lost his first tooth," the proud papa bragged.

"And the tooth fairy paid handsomely, I imagine," she tossed out cheekily, sipping the hot coffee. They both knew government grants didn't make any scientist wealthy. It was their minds, not their bank balances, that were being enriched as they unlocked the mysteries of the polar icepack.

"A silver dollar for the first one."

"Inflation strikes again. Used to be a quarter

several years ago." Kelle spoke with a confidence she didn't feel. The Kleinschmidt boys might be just ordinary middle-class kids, but her own upbringing hadn't even allowed for quarters, much less silver dollars. Foster-care parents watched their nickels and pennies. Food, clothing, and medical expenses were paid for by the government; the tooth fairy was a luxury they couldn't afford.

But Kelle didn't look back with regret. She had carved her own niche in the world. The present and the future were exciting, uncharted roads she looked forward to traveling. She might not have much money, but she loved her work and that alone made her feel rich.

"Yep. How come you aren't stateside having children?"

Kelle laughed at the man's straightforward curiosity. "In answer to your highly personal question," she jibed, "don't you think I ought to find a man first? Not to mention a minister?"

"In all honesty, I'm glad you aren't stateside. You're a damned fine medical man." Laugh lines around his eyes crinkled as he realized his faux pas.

"Thanks." Kelle reached over the table and gave Carroll's freckled hand a friendly pat. His statement gave her a feeling of satisfaction. It reinforced her belief she had been totally accepted as a member of the team. "Speaking of my medical capabilities," she said, glancing at her watch, "I told Mike to report in. Thanks for the coffee, Carroll."

"My pleasure, Doc. By the way, how's Benson's virus?" he inquired before Kelle reached the door.

"Better. Seems to be the three-day infection again. I'm just hoping he doesn't get worse, like Schwartz did." Kelle shrugged.

After six months of isolation, the recurring virus was unexplainable, baffling. Each expedition had faced the same medical problem. It seemed little more than an unusually intense version of the common cold, but it was debilitating and caused quite a few lost man-hours. Fortunately, most members of the current team had avoided the hacking, sore throat and high fever of the virus. Kelle knew she wouldn't be able to find the cure for it any more readily than doctors who had preceded her on such expeditions had. The standard prescription—rest, drink plenty of liquids, and take aspirin to ease discomfort—was the best she could offer.

"Don't let anything get you down here that wouldn't bother you in the States. We've all had bad viruses. Do the same thing you would at home," Carroll said. "Just don't prescribe membership in the Three Hundred Club as an innovative form of treatment."

Kelle laughed and headed out the door. Good advice. Carroll was a perceptive man as well as a scientific genius.

Lengthening her stride, she hurried away from the lounge. She didn't want to think about the Three Hundred Club. She'd decided not to have anything to do with it when the temperature began to hover near the hundred-degree-below mark. Turning the corner, she saw her office door open, but the light wasn't on. "Where the hell is Johnson?" she muttered, exasperated.

"In here, Dr. Langdon."

Stepping inside the door, Kelle flipped on the switch. "Saving electricity?" she demanded, annoyed.

Mike sat on the examining table, long legs swinging his feet a good six inches from the floor. "Nothing to see until you walked in."

"Well, let's take a look at you," Kelle murmured, ignoring his comment.

"No frozen gears. Everything is well oiled and operating smoothly."

For the first time Kelle observed the brown pencil-thin edge circling the blue iris of his eyes. Big *B*, little *b*, she thought, remembering her training in genetics. Pulling her wits together, she said in an uncommonly husky voice, "Indulge my powers of medical observation, please. Let me see your fingertips."

His muscular legs stopped swinging; his knees parted; he held his long fingers out for her inspection. Kelle had no choice but to step between his powerful, trunklike legs and take his hands into her own.

"They look fine," she commented, noting the blunt cut, clean nails, tinged a healthy pink beyond the quick. "How about your toes?"

Mike straightened his legs, locking his knees. "The last time I saw a doctor I was five. The doctor removed my shoes."

Enclosed between the hard strength of his thighs, Kelle gasped inwardly. He had lied. All members of the team had undergone thorough physical examinations as well as psychological profiles. Determined to dislodge the lump at the base of her throat, she swallowed deeply.

"Mr. Johnson, I seriously doubt the doctor who examined you before you joined the team removed your shoes. Would you mind?"

He shrugged his shoulders. "Do your cheeks tingle when they turn that becoming pink?" he teased.

Before she could remove herself from the intimate V his legs had formed, she felt his fingers lightly brush across her cheekbones, then touch the coronet of silver-blond braids wrapped around the crown of her head.

"Your toes," she demanded in a tight, thin voice.

Clearing her throat, she stepped back three spaces. The small office closed in on her. Back to the wall, she heard his throaty laugh, watched him fold one leg on top of the other and remove his shoe.

"You are tingling, aren't you?" he quizzed, the white of his strong even teeth displayed handsomely in stark contrast to his dark moustache and beard.

No longer able to move backward, Kelle sidestepped toward her desk, wanting an immovable object between them. "You're mistaken, Mr. Johnson. I'm merely performing my job . . . just as you did earlier."

His shoe thudding to the floor, Mike got off the table and sauntered toward the desk. She noticed his blue eyes narrowing speculatively. "Were you performing your job when I felt your body quiver against mine? Did your thumbs—"

"Mr. Johnson!" Kelle interrupted, searching wildly for an appropriate putdown.

"Mike," he corrected. "You'd be lying through your teeth if you denied that you felt something."

"Mike. You're mistaken, not to mention way out of line," she began.

"Am I? Sit down, Kelle."

His authoritative manner momentarily made Kelle comply with the command. Her own fear made her angry. He might be twice her size, but he wasn't going to intimidate Dr. Kelle Langdon. Abruptly she rose and quickly regretted her impetuous motion.

Palms flat, arms braced on the desk, he stared at the shadowed rise and fall of her breasts. His jaw firmed, resulting in a slight, momentary twitch. Kelle sank back down. Their eyes met.

"Your medical education should have taught you a few basic facts. For example, normal healthy men and women locked up together for months in this icy wilderness would eventually feel a natural attraction for each other. I'm right, aren't I?"

"Absolutely not," she denied, eyes wide, shocked at the implication in his words.

"No?"

"No," Kelle echoed in what she hoped was a firm voice. Her heart was beating furiously. She thought he was going to prove how wrong she was when he bent across the wooden desk. He's going to kiss me, she thought in a panic, and then was appalled by the disappointment she felt when he slowly straightened.

His dark eyebrow raised, marking his disbelief. "I don't believe you're being honest with yourself, Dr. Langdon, and I don't believe I'm wrong."

As casually as he had approached the desk, he retreated. Stooping, he picked up his shoe and nonchalantly strolled to the doorway.

"Think about it."

Kelle didn't realize she'd been holding her breath, but the second Mike was gone, she exhaled deeply. She suddenly felt as if she had a high fever, as if her entire body was ablaze.

Oh, God, I must be coming down with the virus, she thought, unwilling to admit the obvious. Mentally she began ticking off her symptoms: accelerated heartbeat, upset stomach, slight temperature, spells of dizziness, dry mouth, jerky coordination. Didn't sound like a cold, she quickly surmised. Sounds like . . . no! She shook her head vehemently. It's not possible.

Analyze the data, she thought, trying as best she could to remain completely rational. It couldn't have been that man who had had such a profound effect on her. She couldn't afford any emotional entanglements here. Besides, he had as much as said that he was only attracted to her because she was the only woman available.

Leaning back in her swivel chair, she brushed her fingertips back and forth across her forehead, as her glasses slipped down her nose. Impatiently she flung them on the desk. She didn't need Mike Johnson to tell her she had to be the only woman around before he would take a second look at her. He knew his tall, dark, handsome looks would turn female heads anywhere. She was perfectly aware that she was not as beautiful or as attractive as the women he was used to.

Kelle prided herself on being a realist. She knew it was always better to face facts than to take refuge in fantasy. She would never have a chance with a man like Mike. She would have to accept that fact and go on as before.

"Beauty from within is more important than superficial beauty," she stated aloud, quoting her foster mother.

Inner beauty had been slow to bloom also. But by the time she had completed her medical degree she could stand, shoulders straight, chin thrust forward, ready to shine. Why did Mike Johnson have to come into her well-ordered life and upset her equilibrium? She'd taught herself self-sufficiency. She didn't want to test the weakest link in a psychologically strong chain.

Kelle consoled herself with the thought that she would soon be rid of Mike Johnson forever. At the most they would be confined to the South Pole for another few weeks. She wouldn't allow herself to notice the treacherous betrayals of her body. To her they would be as devoid of substance as the mirages Scott and Amundsen had experienced when they trudged toward the Pole.

"You have other goals to focus on," she reminded herself. "The spacelab."

Kelle opened the center drawer and pulled out the study she had been compiling on the effects of long periods of isolation on humans. With her background, a shot of luck, and a well-compiled report, perhaps she'd be considered for the spacelab.

When she found she couldn't tally up a line of figures properly, she realized she wasn't succeeding in blocking Mike Johnson from her mind. Raising her head, she could almost see him, smell him, touch the image so clearly imprinted on her mind. A compelling pair of blue eyes outlined in brown told her she faced a hard, lonely struggle. Stifling a sigh, she wondered what it would feel like not to fight her feelings, but to surrender to them.

Mike Johnson stopped in the hallway to slip his shoe back on and tie it, a self-satisfied smile on his face. He'd done it. He'd finally worked up the courage to speak frankly to Dr. Langdon.

"It only took me six months," he mouthed sarcastically.

But he'd secretly watched her during that time. He'd observed the feminine curves hidden beneath the blue jeans and bulky wool shirts. He had long denied himself the pleasure of reaching out and touching her shining platinum hair. Her voice seemed like tinkling wind chimes compared to the lower masculine laughter of the men.

He knew Kelle prided herself on being friendly and impartial with everyone, himself included. He also knew she worked hard to make the men on the expedition consider her just one of the boys. Perhaps that was a necessary defense in a situation such as this, Mike realized, but something had happened outside. He couldn't explain it; it wasn't scientific, but it was there. Intuitively he'd known she had reacted to him as a woman does to a man. He hadn't imagined it, he reassured himself. She had trembled. She had been unsure of herself, of him, and had quickly withdrawn.

Could I be wrong? he wondered. It had been six months since he'd seen another woman. Was he letting sexual demands outweigh common sense? He shook his shaggy head. If he was mistaken, as she claimed, it wasn't because their bodies didn't respond to each other. She might say that he meant nothing to her, but on a gut level, he was certain she felt something toward him.

He remembered the softness of her hands as they clasped his lightly. The memory merged with an old, forgotten memory from the past. He'd been what, eighteen, nineteen? Madly infatuated with the most popular girl in the senior class, he remembered cruising around her house in his souped-up Ford for months before he had managed to speak to her. Oh, he knew Carolyn had shrewdly given him the once-over. How could she miss a boy who stood head and shoulders over most of their classmates? It wasn't as though he'd ever been inconspicuous in a crowd. Her brown eyes had seemed to caress him, he recalled. She was curious; he was shy. He worshipped her; she thought of him as just another boy in her class.

Mike grimaced, wishing he hadn't dredged up a painful memory from the past. Pristine Carolyn had hurt him deeply with her coy "Don't touch me, your hands are greasy" routine. He'd never made that mistake again, he recalled, congratulating himself.

Was he about to with Kelle? Did she want to use him? Inwardly Mike cringed. Damn it to hell, he silently cursed. Kelle wasn't like Carolyn . . . or was she? Was he halfway in love with a woman who could reopen an old wound? No! his mind rebelled. It wasn't the same. But even Kelle had seen him for what he was: a glorified grease monkey.

Mike Johnson was blue collar and Dr. Kelle Langdon was strictly starched white collar. Maybe he was crazy to expect her to feel any attraction for him. In an emotional muddle, he felt as though he had stumbled back out into the Antarctic cold in the midst of a whiteout. Blind reason wouldn't get him back to safety. He'd have to wait until the storm died down.

Snorting to himself, he wondered if Kelle would respond to him if they were back home in the States. Probably not, he decided, unless she needed her car fixed.

## *CHAPTER TWO*

It was virtually impossible not to see Mike in the days that followed, but Kelle did her best to keep their encounters polite and businesslike.

On the first night at dinner, she'd been forced to ask him to pass the milk or drink her coffee black. She had wanted to avoid touching his large hands but knew that would have been impossible. Kelle cursed herself silently when she saw her own hand visibly shaking, and to make matters almost unbearable, she had actually dropped the bowl. The suppressed amusement lurking in his blue eyes was unmistakable and infuriating. By the third day, Mike haunted her. She was beginning to feel as if he was hovering around her . . . constantly. By bedtime her nerves were screaming for a confrontation.

But what could she accuse him of? Lurking in corners? Solicitously getting her a cup of coffee when she returned from taking a reading on equipment outside the dome? Attempting to beat her at the evening dart game? Any comment she could make would only be interpreted as shrewish if overheard by other members of the team.

How many times had she asked herself if she was slightly paranoid? Or was she simply oversensitive to one particular man? After all, he seldom spoke. His eyes said it all.

She could almost hear his thoughts. Do you wear glasses all the time? he seemed to be asking when she stopped the dart game to clean them. His eyes scrutinized the braids piled on her head, and he seemed to be wondering about her hair's length. When she spoke his eyes hungrily watched her lips. Are they soft? Moist? Welcoming?

More infuriating than his silent questions was her desire to ask questions of her own. Had he always had a beard? Would it prickle or be soft if she stroked it? What would he look like without it?

Kelle also found herself watching him while he interacted with other members of the staff. His quiet confidence, his ability to listen to others, his unassuming manner impressed her tremendously. Everyone admired and respected him. Kelle, to her own chagrin, realized she was no exception.

Alone in her office, desperately trying to understand her own emotional response to Mike, Kelle paced back and forth. Could she have been subconsciously aware of him throughout the long winter months? Had what happened in the dome been the accumulation of some hidden female frustration? No! she wanted to shout. He's just testing me like he would one of his damned engines. Reluctantly she realized she was at the point of giving in unless she could search through her medicine cabinet and find a prescription for self-control. That certainly had been in short supply the previous night in the recreation room.

Mike seldom played bridge, but he nonchalantly filled the empty chair across from Kelle when her partner excused himself.

"Who's winning?" he asked as he picked up each card being dealt by the director, Dr. Ivan Svensky.

"Your opponents are ahead by two games," Carroll replied, letting his cards pile up in front of him.

Mike grinned. "Guess you need a new partner, huh?"

"Nobody beats these two card sharks," Kelle answered noncommittally.

His knees touched hers; she jerked back in her chair. Her eyes were icy cold as she looked across the width of the oblong table. For a moment she wanted to run away as his canvas-covered feet lightly captured hers between them. Ivan and Carroll's feet weren't anywhere within reach.

His smile informed her he wasn't about to release her. His dark brow rose slightly as he softly increased the pressure of his calves on hers as though asking, Going to cause a scene in front of the director?

Kelle shook her head slightly in reply. Let him play the hand, she thought. Once his energies were directed toward concentrating on the cards, she'd extricate herself from his touch.

A wide smile crossed her face when she viewed the aces and face cards she had been dealt. Considering that she hadn't had more than four points the entire evening, she wondered begrudgingly if the change in partners had also changed her luck.

Ivan passed. With a wicked gleam in her eye, Kelle bid two no trump, asking for her partner's longest and strongest suit. Once he mentioned a suit she planned on running him right on up to game level.

"By me," Carroll bid as he glanced at Kelle.

"Two hearts," Mike responded.

"Insufficient bid," Kelle blurted out, secretly delighted that he knew so little about the value of the cards. She'd have no trouble beating him at this game.

Mike tapped his cards with one finger, then he leveled his penetrating gaze on her. "Six hearts enough?"

"Small slam?" Ivan asked, a flicker of amusement twitching his lips upward. "You don't mess around, do you?"

Kelle nearly dropped her cards when she heard Mike reply in an innocent tone, "Not usually. I play to win."

She felt the tip of his toe climb from her ankle, up her calf, then playfully tickle the back of her knees. Get control, she warned herself firmly, gritting her teeth to still the infuriating tremor in her hands. Goosebumps began to rise on her arms and Kelle's cards blurred before her eyes.

"Seven hearts," she overbid in a voice higher than normal.

"Gutsy," Carroll responded, thumping his cards, "but I don't think you can make it. I'll double."

The hidden message behind Mike's redouble left little doubt in her mind that he intended to win more than a game of cards. His arrogant self-assurance made her heart rate increase dramatically. Could a novice player possibly make a grand slam?

Ivan passed, tossing out a low club to initiate the lead. Unable to comment, swallowing deeply, Kelle spread her cards out for her partner's scrutiny. Mike would play both hands; she was dummy. She watched as Mike slid the nine of clubs over his opponent's card.

"Your deep finesse will never work," Carroll said, bluffing.

Mike stared into her eyes. Was his amused smile his way of telling her that the past few days he had been practicing finesse with her? Was he as confident of winning her as he was the card game? Kelle shivered inwardly when his toe traveled a sensuous path up her leg.

She cleared her throat loudly and moved her feet behind the rungs of her chair.

Card by card Mike led and captured the first dozen tricks. Soon his opponents were squirming in their seats, trying to figure out what to hold on to and what to discard.

"You made it!" Kelle whispered when the last card had been played. She was certain she wouldn't have been able to do the same.

Ivan clapped Mike on the shoulder. "Something tells me this wasn't beginner's luck. Where did you learn to play like this? Why haven't you joined us before now?"

"The first book my grandmother taught me to read was *Goren's Beginner's Bridge*," he replied, chuckling. "I'm also extremely lucky with pasteboards."

"So you'd rather fleece the poker players than play bridge?" Carroll joked as he gathered the playing cards. "We could play for a tenth of a cent a point if it would make the game more interesting."

Mike shook his head. "I'd end up owning your oldest child," he quipped, "and I'd hate to see your boy raised in a motherless home." The glance he shot Kelle told her he played to win, but with good conscience.

"I'm not putting my hard-earned money out there," Ivan protested. "I've always maintained I'd rather have luck than skill."

"How wonderful to have both," Kelle commented, unaware she had spoken the words aloud until she saw a red tide of color staining the cheekbones above Mike's dark beard.

She realized she had embarrassed him with her open praise. He could laugh and tease about winning the hand, but he had difficulty accepting her compliment. For a moment she gained insight into his personality. Humility and self-assuredness seemed to balance each other.

As she picked up the cards to shuffle them, she caught herself smiling when Mike stretched out his legs and tapped out a happy rhythm on the top of her shoe. Without thinking, she unhooked her legs from the rung of the chair and moved them back under the table. Mike squeezed his legs together lightly. She grinned at the face cards she picked up, accepting her good hand and the fact that she now knew she truly liked the hunk of a man sitting across the table from her.

Later, the cards put away, Mike accompanied her back to her quarters near the infirmary. Neither of them spoke. Both seemed inhibited by being alone instead of having others surround them.

"Thanks for breaking Ivan and Carroll's winning streak," she babbled in an effort to fill the silence.

"My pleasure."

"I can't remember having such spectacular cards dealt to me," she continued inanely.

Mike cut through the chatter by touching her. A few strands of hair had escaped from her braids and dangled beside her ear. Before he tucked it behind her ear, he rubbed it between his thumb and forefinger as though he could capture the silvery highlights and keep them in the hand he plunged into his pocket.

Struggling to establish a casual camaraderie, Kelle yawned. Her jaw popped indelicately beneath the hand she had politely used to cover her mouth. Outside her door, her heart thudding in her chest when she saw the intensity in Mike's eyes, she stopped struggling with the inevitable.

"Back in Houston you'd ask me to come in for a cup of coffee, wouldn't you?"

"Texas is a long, long way from the South Pole," she answered, wondering what it felt like to kiss a man with a full beard.

Mike shifted his weight to one leg, crossing his ankles, and leaned against the doorjamb. Was now the time to risk a finesse and possibly lose the queen, he wondered, or should I play it safe and hope the card would fall later in the game? The chance of winning wasn't great enough. He'd play the odds.

"Well, lady, we both have a busy day tomorrow. Sweet dreams."

He didn't wait for a response; he pivoted quickly and strode toward his own quarters.

Kelle was left with her jaw hanging. Doesn't he know I expected a good-night kiss? she thought. When she entered her quarters her disappointment was darker than the unlit room. The door latch clinking behind her brought her to her senses.

But the next morning, pacing like a caged animal, fretting over what had and had not taken place, Kelle wondered if the isolation was finally getting to her. She had better sense than to invite physical intimacies with one of the men. Hadn't she spent the first month at the camp establishing her self-sufficient image? Hadn't she rebuffed all the subtle advances from the men who had originally considered her the only fair game in an uncharted territory?

Hands on her hips, irked by the muddle of emotions she found herself in, she ignored a voice calling her name.

"Kelle?"

She heard her name called again, followed by three sharp raps on her closed door. "Yes," she responded automatically, opening the door.

Carroll, a worried frown creasing his brow, entered the room. "We need your help. Can you spare a couple of hours?"

"Sure. What's wrong?"

"We're getting some unusual readings on the seismograph. Schwartz, Petersen, and I are interpreting the readings, but we need someone to monitor the equipment. Do you mind?"

"Of course not. What exactly do you want me to do?"

"Just give us a reading every twenty minutes or so," Carroll answered, heading back out the door toward the workroom.

Kelle turned in the opposite direction and hurried toward the equipment room. A sense of urgency seemed to hover like a gray cloud. She turned and glanced backward when she heard footsteps from behind.

"Mike! Where are you going?"

"I've been assigned to assist you. Relay the readings to the workroom. They don't want any time gaps."

He closed the gap between them with long strides. Shoulders brushing as they continued down the narrow hallway, Kelle's stomach tightened. They were going to be alone, together, isolated from the others. She feared each step took them closer and closer to something that frightened her very much.

Mike opened the door and waited for Kelle to enter. With a searching look into his eyes, she walked in ahead of him. The room held an array of technical apparatus, but Kelle strode purposefully toward the graph-producing machine in the back of the crowded room.

The short hairs on the back of her neck, pulled taut by the circle of braids wrapped around her head, tightened as she bowed her head to watch the needle on the seismograph slowly move up and down. Automatically she tugged at her hair, loosening the pressure. She wasn't aware of the seductiveness of the gesture until she heard Mike's swift intake of air.

"I'll get you a stool," he said softly.

She nodded gratefully, not certain how long

her knees could support her weight while under his scrutiny.

"Do you know how to read these?" she asked, breaking the silence and pointing toward the black peaks and valleys on the page.

The moment the inane question passed her lips, she knew she'd made a tactical error. Mike moved closer. His warm breath stirred the wisps of hair by her ear. When he told her he didn't she could smell the minty fragrance of his breath.

"I'm no expert," she began nervously chattering, "but . . ." His curved finger brushed the silver-blond strand of hair behind her ear. "Mike . . ." She could hear the panic in her voice but couldn't restrain it.

"Kelle . . . ?"

She searched his face frantically, trying to fathom his intent. The dark rim around his iris made the blue seem piercing. Gently his hand started to remove her glasses.

"I can't see very well without them," she protested. Her hands raised to stop him, but they didn't raise higher than his muscular chest. "Oh, Mike. Please. Don't."

"A kiss, Kelle. Maybe the first at the South Pole. Without these."

She heard the sound of glasses being carefully set on the metal cover of the seismograph. Her vision blurred; Mike's features became fuzzy. His hands lightly caressed her upper arms, turning her pliant body toward his.

"I know it won't work in the long run," he muttered, gently cupping the sides of her face, "but I need this kiss . . . badly."

Lighter than a snowflake, his mouth covered hers. There was a reverence in his touch Kelle didn't understand. She envisioned them standing alone in a tall pine forest, the soft snow of winter with a whispering sigh falling about them, separating them from mankind. Isolation at its best.

This wasn't Kelle's first kiss; she'd experienced the hard biting pressure of desire. But this kiss was as different as the man she shared it with. It was tender, making Kelle feel cherished . . . for the first time in her life.

It ended as it began, with a soft sigh from both of them.

"Kelle . . . Kelle," Mike whispered. One kiss hadn't quenched his need. But he had promised himself to be content with it. He'd worshipped her from afar; he didn't want to spoil it in any way.

"You shouldn't have done that," Kelle whispered, then gradually opened her eyes.

Mike lowered his hands to the curve of her shoulders and drew her close. "I'll remember it always," he promised in a husky tone. The tips of her golden eyelashes fluttered against the softness of his beard. But she didn't withdraw as he had expected.

"This is wrong. We shouldn't have—"

"Shh. Shhh. You can't tell me anything beautiful can be wrong. I'm not poetic, Kelle. I wish I could say all the words to convince you this is more than a passing fancy . . . or just a physical need. I can't." His hands soothingly stroked her hair. Searching desperately for something to say, he began, "To me it's like tuning up a race car, turning on the ignition and listening to the engine purr, then fantasizing about winning the Indianapolis Five Hundred." He groaned at comparing Kelle to a fast, sleek race car. No woman wants to be compared to a cold piece of machinery, he thought morosely.

Kelle smiled at his analogy but she understood what he meant. She had experienced the same feelings the first time she'd seen a child born. But she wasn't about to relate the incident. The last thing a man wanted to hear when he kissed a woman was a monologue about babies. Silently she cursed herself for being clumsy and awkward in his light embrace. In her entire lifetime, no one had ever held her with such loving care.

"Your beard is soft," she murmured against his chest, saying the next thought that came into her head.

"Your hair is softer. I'd like to see it loose. I'll

bet it's like a"—Mike paused, considering—"a silk cloud." He searched wildly for less trite phrases to tell her how beautiful she was, but couldn't find them. It was hell having her in his arms, wanting to tell her how fantastic she was, and suffering from paralysis of the brain. The lady doctor and the grease jockey, he thought, mentally whipping himself.

"We'd better check the readings," he suggested softly, knowing his self-control was slipping when he felt the tips of her breasts through the thickness of his shirt.

Kelle stepped away instantly, blindly groping for her glasses. "Yes. The readings."

"Your glasses," Mike said as he slid them back in place. "See anything interesting?" Why, he wondered, can my tongue agilely tease her, provoke her, then get twisted into a knot when I want to speak to her?

Seeing the misery in his eyes, in such stark contrast to the devilish grin on his face, Kelle suddenly realized he was as nervous as she was. But why? He must be used to women standing in line waiting for him.

Impulsively she reached up, her fingertips brushing his moustache. "I see a handsome devil in blue jeans who is *very* distracting."

"And I see the most beautiful doctor in the world."

"I'll file that information for future reference, Mr. Johnson. We'll see if you still think so once we're back in the States."

"Is there going to be a future, Dr. Langdon?" He knew he shouldn't have asked, but he needed to know if the kiss was a beginning or an end.

Kelle braced herself against the machine, momentarily mesmerized by the movements of the needle. "Mike, I'll admit we're attracted to each other, but . . . what will happen when we leave the Pole?" *I'll no longer be the only woman in an all-male environment.*

"Are you admitting to lusting after my body?" Mike asked in an effort to inject the light tone back into their conversation. He didn't want to hear another rejection from her and knew he would have to change the direction of the conversation fast. "You can't seduce me. I'm a virgin," he teased, uttering the first outlandish thing entering his mind.

Laughing softly, Kelle tried to give the appearance of avidly concentrating on the graph. "I think you'll be safe."

"That's what I'm afraid of," Mike muttered quietly as he pulled two stools over for them to sit down on. "So tell me. What's a nice girl like you doing in a polar icebox?"

"Seducing innocent virgins," Kelle quipped. She watched his dark eyebrow raise, then added in a mockingly serious tone, "And keeping the polar bears away."

"There aren't any polar bears at the South Pole."

"See what a great job I'm doing?"

Together they chuckled at the twist of an age-old joke.

"What do you attribute your success to, Dr. Langdon?" Mike asked. He wanted to keep her laughing long enough for it to become a permanent imprint on his mind. Tonight, when he was alone, and lonely, he'd remember it . . . and the kiss.

"Garlic. Sure-fire means of keeping lecherous men and polar bears away. Haven't you noticed? None of the men have even attempted to break into my room."

"You're sure it's the garlic?"

Kelle nodded her head enthusiastically, then covered her insecurity with a radiant false smile. "Without the garlic none of you would be able to resist my raving beauty, my charming wit, my—"

"Locked door?"

"There isn't a lock on my door," Kelle blurted. A tide of red flushed from her collarbone to her hairline. My God, that sounded like an open invitation. "See . . . the garlic works every time." Tears of shame began collecting in the corners of her eyes. She'd tried to keep the conversation frivolous. Why did she feel like crying? Hands trembling, she ripped off the sheets and removed them from the wire seismograph basket. "You'd better take these to the workroom."

"Kelle, what's wrong?"

"Nothing, but we're late with these. The mad scientists will toss you out into the cold if you don't get going."

"Did I say something? Do something wrong?" She looked like she was about to cry and he didn't know why. A single tear trickled down her cheek before she ducked her head away from him.

"It's nothing. Eye strain," she muttered, coming up with the first excuse she could think of. "Go on. Get out of here," she whispered.

Mike reached for her trembling shoulders. Inches away from comforting her he stopped. He didn't know whether to gather her into his arms and kiss away the tears or follow her orders. With great hesitation, he picked up the graph papers and headed toward the door. As he was about to step into the hallway, he paused, turning back toward the solitary woman bent over the machine.

"Kelle. I love garlic." Quietly he closed the door behind himself.

Mike wended his way through the short maze of aluminum tunnels until he turned into the workroom. With each step he cursed himself for ineptness. What had he done to make Kelle cry? He hadn't forced the kiss on her. She hadn't wrapped her arms around his waist as he had fantasized, but she hadn't recoiled either. Her lips hadn't been stiff, unyielding, had they?

"Johnson, you look like you've been mowed down by a snowmobile. There isn't anything wrong with the equipment, is there?" Carroll asked when he saw Mike enter the room.

Handing the stack of printouts to Carroll, he silently nodded his head. "Guess I'm concerned about your hypothesis. Do you really think volcanic eruptions in North America will result in earthquakes around the globe?"

"It's an educated guess. Not a fact." Worried lines creased Carroll's forehead. "Mother Nature is tricky. We may not see indications of the shifting of the crust of the earth; we may see a radical change in weather patterns instead."

Although Schwartz appeared buried shoulder deep in maps, Mike heard him snort, then chuckle. "Yesterday he told us about the tooth fairy visiting his son; today it's Mother Nature. Carroll, are you certain you aren't an impostor masquerading as a scientist?"

The tension eased as the men laughed at the goodnatured jibe.

"Notice how all his fantasies are about

women?" Schwartz added. "Good thing there's a shortage of them down here."

"What about Dr. Langdon?" Carroll noted. "Have you forgotten how to identify them?"

"Guess I forget about her being a woman sometimes. Good thing too. Anybody caught eyeing her gets a double dose of saltpeter in their mashed potatoes. Thank goodness she hasn't caused any trouble. There are times, gentlemen, when I sorely miss my wife." Schwartz stopped turning through the pages. "Hey, Petersen, look at this!"

Mike left the room unnoticed as the three men rapidly flipped through the remaining printouts. His fingers traced over his upper lip as he recalled the pleasure of kissing Kelle. What would the effect have been on the men had he personally testified to Dr. Langdon being all woman? It would definitely cause a problem, he realized. Although a woman, any woman, would be offended by Schwartz's forgetfulness, he realized what a difficult position Kelle had been in all these months. Any sort of relationship between Kelle and him could cause her endless problems.

By the time Mike returned, Kelle had herself under control. She had enjoyed Mike's kiss more than she would admit, even to herself, but she knew it could never be repeated. Kelle wasn't about to set herself up for heartbreak just because Mike was attractive. She'd have to toughen up, freeze him out, or she'd return to the States a sadder but much wiser woman. Exploring the world of sexual delights wasn't on the approved government grant list!

The door had barely shut when Mike said, "Kelle, we need to talk." She turned to him, her expression calm and emotionless. She couldn't let him know she had been thinking about him. "I'd be putting you in danger if I openly courted you," he began in a direct manner. "You're the only woman surrounded by nineteen men who have been cooped up here for six months."

And one passionless kiss didn't excite you enough to warrant further intimacies, Kelle silently acknowledged.

"I told you your virginity is safe. What do you want? A signed, notarized affidavit?" Kelle retorted waspishly.

"You don't understand. . . ."

"Look, Mike. I didn't ask for the kiss. Sorry it was such a disappointment, but if you'll recall, *I* told *you* any type of relationship between us wouldn't work." Kelle rose to her feet in what she hoped was a regal manner. "We'd be worlds apart if we were in a normal situation. Let's just forget it, shall we?"

Mike's hurt quickly changed to anger at her words. "Don't pull the haughty Ice Queen routine with me, Lady. If we were in a normal situation I'd kiss you senseless."

"What makes you think I'd ever let you near me if we were in a normal situation?" she spat at him, her blue eyes scathingly raked over his muscular body. "Don't overestimate yourself. I don't need you or any other man."

Step by step Mike closed the gap between them. "For a doctor, you don't know much about biology. It's time you learned that making love isn't a mental exercise."

"Making love? I have no intention of—"

"Neither did I until now," Mike said ominously. "It's time somebody gave you an explicit lesson."

"Don't touch me . . . you . . . you . . ." Kelle sputtered, searching for savage putdown. "You animal!" she said just as his hands clamped on her arms, pinning them to her sides, then slid to her back, arching her against him.

Rage blinded Mike. Angrily he ground his mouth against hers to stop any further demeaning epithets. *Animal!* his mind shrieked. She'd fooled him with her demure protestations earlier. His mouth rocked back and forth, grinding his beard across her chin. He was determined to dominate her spiteful tongue with his own. Clamped against his torso, she struggled to free herself but he captured her buttocks in his hands and ground her hips erotically against his own. Her jaw slackened; his tongue surged forward. The honeyed moisture of the interior of her mouth soothed the angry fires burning behind the lids of his eyes.

*Damn it, respond,* he mentally ordered. Slowly he began coaxing reciprocation by easing the pressure. Seductively his tongue probed her mouth, as he willed her to match his provocative strokes. He heard a small groan from deep in her throat and felt the tenseness slowly leaving her rigid body. A feeling of triumph surged through him and he felt his body react fully to hers. Her voluptuous softness enticed him; she goaded him into mindless fantasy.

He wanted more than response. He wanted participation. He wanted to feel her hands curl around his shoulders, digging into the muscles of his back with abandon. He wanted her to wrap her legs around his waist. He wanted to feel her welcoming moistness enveloping him. Lost in passion, he cradled Kelle against him in a parody of lovemaking, letting her feel the explicit proof of his desire.

A small whimpering sound, the taste of salt, a dampness on her cheeks broke through his sensuous fantasy. Shame overwhelmed him. Disgust with himself obliterated the dream. *God! Have I lost my mind?*

Abruptly he released Kelle, then turned and hurried out of the room.

Kelle slumped to the wooden floor. Shakily she rubbed the palms of her hands over her face. She had done her best to fight him and lost. Tears were streaming down her face. Mike Johnson had succeeded . . . he'd awakened her dormant passion and when he had become aware of his victory, he had abandoned her. Mortified by her lack of control, she covered her face with both hands, seeking to hide her shame.

But her body wouldn't allow easy forgetfulness. The tips of her breasts ached, as did the lower portion of her body. She drew her knees up and buried her face against the coarse fabric of her jeans. "What am I going to do?" she moaned, rocking back and forth. He knew she wanted him. And more degrading, when he had found out, he'd left!

"Your fault, you inexperienced fool," she muttered aloud. "I challenged him. Dared him to prove himself as a man. What did I expect?"

Only the hum of the equipment answered her questions. Beyond hearing anything, feeling anything other than disgust, she rose to her feet. Eyes vacant, she stared at the smoothly operating machinery.

I'll have to avoid him, she decided. She couldn't trust herself around him. She wouldn't ever let him humiliate her again. Kelle wiped her damp cheeks. Pull yourself together, she instructed. Only Mike knows of your pitiful sins and he won't tell . . . or will he?

Kelle sniffed. The final humiliation would be having the men she worked with know what had happened. But somehow, intuitively, she knew Mike didn't need to brag about his conquest. The only way they would find out was if she babbled about the indiscretion. Tucking her shirttail back in place, lightly running her hands over her hair, she wished she had a mirror to assess the damage.

"Kelle?" Her name being called over the squawk box made her jerk her head upward.

"Yes, Carroll," she responded carefully after she'd pushed the black button on the wall that connected to the speaker system.

"You and Mike can go on about your other duties. We've found the information we needed in the last batch of graphs."

"Anything specific?" she asked, thankful she wasn't going to have to make up an excuse for delivering the next graphs herself.

"Nothing that hasn't been discovered long ago."

Kelle could hear the disappointment in his voice. "Sorry, Carroll."

"Thanks anyway for your help."

"No problem," she responded automatically. "If you need me again, I'll be in my office."

"Roger."

Kelle ran her hands down the side of her jeans, then opened the door. "No problem?" she repeated, her voice filled with irony. "My problems are too numerous to list! And Mike Johnson is at the top."

## CHAPTER THREE

Kelle paused at the door of the dining room a few seconds and listened to the conversation. The men bantered jovially about turning the sauna up to prepare for the initiation into the Three Hundred Club. To join you had to run naked into the snow when the temperature was at least one hundred degrees below zero. Excitement at the prospect made their laughter louder than normal.

Kelle entered the room unobtrusively. She seated herself at a table for eight, carefully noting she wasn't the last to arrive. Mike wasn't there yet.

"Pass the fish, please," she requested in a subdued voice once she had seated herself.

"Don't eat too much. Everything in your

stomach is going to flash-freeze when you run out into the snow," one of the men teased as he handed her the platter.

"You're going to catch pneumonia. Benson's germs are skulking in the corners waiting for anybody crazy enough to tempt them." Kelle knew it was hopeless to order them to stay inside, but she considered their preoccupation with the Three Hundred Club to be absurd.

"Don't tell me you're going to chicken out," Carroll admonished lightly. "This is something to brag about to your grandchildren!"

"Hey, Mike! Ready for a reckless dash into the freezer? Petersen says the temperature is steadily dropping."

The only seat vacant was at Kelle's table. "I'm game," he answered, noting the stiff erectness of her back. Trying to act normally, he pulled out the empty chair and sat down. Don't look at her, he warned himself, afraid of the silent recriminations he would see in her face.

"Don't worry about those big, bad germs," Petersen kidded, pointing the tongs of his fork in her direction. "Scientifically they can't exist in this environment. Therefore they are a figment of your medical imagination."

"Tell it to Benson. He's the one imagining the sore throat and dripping nose," Kelle retorted. "I'm advising against it."

"Have a heart, Doc. This is one of the highlights of being here," one of the support staff argued.

Petersen leaned forward and whispered loudly, "Are the rumors true, Kelle? Did they really find various anatomical parts shriveled up and slowly thawing outside the front door during the summer expedition?"

Kelle grinned, refusing to let the blood rush to her face. One of the prices for being "one of the boys" was accepting their good-natured teasing. "Oh, dear," she replied in an equally loud whisper. "I hoped you guys wouldn't hear that rumor. It's true. There were several . . . casualties last year. But that's the bad news. The good news is they all made it into the Polar Boys' Choir."

The room resounded with boisterous laughter. Several men slapped each other on the backs at her remarks.

"She always gives as good as she gets," Carroll shouted with glee.

Beneath her fringe of long eyelashes she glanced at Mike's face in time to see him wipe his nose and tuck the tissue in his pocket.

"Mike? Are you feeling well?" she asked.

Eyes glued to his plate, he answered, "Nothing to worry about, Dr. Langdon."

"Don't worry, Doc," she heard, "he's going to freeze every one of those germs!"

Kelle wheeled around in her chair. "Is there anyone else with viral symptoms?" She scanned each man's face. "Sheer insanity to romp outside if you do," she warned.

"We're hale and hearty. Stop fussing," one of the geophysicists scoffed. "Damn it, Kelle. There are times when you act like an old woman."

"Using good sense doesn't make me an old woman," she retorted. To take the sting out of the rebuke she added, "Even though I am older than you are."

"And you definitely can't deny being a woman," the geophysicist rebutted.

Five long seconds of silence passed as all eyes shifted in her direction. It was as if the men had only now become aware of her gender.

"Pass the corn, please," Mike requested hoarsely in an effort to reestablish the equilibrium. "I didn't check the message board. Did anything come over the radio for me today?"

"You didn't get your torrid message for the day?" Carroll asked in mock horror.

Nervous laughter broke through the tension. Normal conversations resumed. Mike had drawn the attention away from Kelle and focused it on himself. Kelle chewed a bite of fish until she thought it could safely slide past through her constricted throat. Mike had every reason to be disgusted with her, but he'd gallantly diverted any verbal speculation as to whether or not she, a woman, would be joining the rites attached to the Three Hundred Club.

How could she convince him not to participate in this ridiculous event? If he was coming down with the virus, the last thing he should do is expose himself to any drastic change in temperature. The topic of conversation had switched and she dreaded the thought of drawing any attention to herself.

Mechanically she ate her meal while keeping her eye on Mike. Not once did he glance in her direction. He shoved his food from one side of the plate to the other as if he had no appetite. He'd probably weakened his immune system that day in the dome when he'd been chilled to the bone, Kelle thought.

Maybe I should take him aside and advise him against subjecting his body to any unwarranted dangers. Take him aside? she jeered. He's so repulsed he can't even look at you!

"More fish?" Carroll offered, extending the nearly empty platter in her direction.

"Huh?"

"Stop woolgathering, Kelle. Are you really worried about these crazy lunatics' health?"

"You're all grown men. You know the risks." Kelle shrugged but was surprised by the simple solution. If Mike decided he wanted to risk his health by dashing naked into the cold, there wasn't a single thing she could do about it.

"It'll be okay," Carroll reassured her. His voice lowered. "But I think you should retire early, hmm?"

Kelle saw the wisdom in his suggestion and complied with a nod of her head and a crisp, "Excuse me."

Walking toward her room, she remembered at one time thinking about making a mad dash into the cold darkness herself. Other women were members of the Three Hundred Club. However, she reminded herself, they weren't the *only* woman wintering over. Her case was different, especially after that glaring reminder during dinner. To go through the initiation would be the most foolish thing she could do.

Loud masculine whoops echoed from the other room. Undoubtedly the temperature had dropped to the required reading. She listened carefully for Mike's voice and didn't hear it.

"Stay in out of the cold," she muttered. "For my sake, don't be foolish!"

In her room she flopped on her bed and picked up the novel she kept by the bedside. She had a hard time concentrating on the story, but eventually she found herself relaxing deeply. Before she realized it her eyes closed and the book fell out of her hand.

Awakening with a start, Kelle glanced at the bedside clock. She was shocked to discover it was after midnight.

"Kelle . . . are you asleep?"

Softly someone rapped on her door.

"Who is it?"

"Carroll."

"Just a minute." Swinging her legs off the bed, Kelle yawned, stretched, then bid him to come in.

"Sorry to wake you, but I think we have a sick man on our hands."

Instantly alert, Kelle demanded, "Who?"

"Mike Johnson. I had to threaten him with bodily harm to get him to the infirmary, but he's there waiting for you."

"Was he stupid enough to go outside?" she demanded harshly.

Hangdog expression on his face, Carroll nodded.

"The damned fool. Why didn't you . . . ? Never mind! I guess I should have expected it. At least Benson's well enough to be back to work now." Exasperation was evident in her voice. "What are his symptoms?"

Together they rushed out of her room toward the isolation infirmary adjoining her office. Carroll ticked off the same symptoms she'd listed on Benson's chart: fever, sore throat, headache, coughing.

"You go back to bed, Carroll. I can manage."

"Kelle, I feel guilty as hell. He wasn't going to join the club until a few of us teased him about being the mechanic with no antifreeze in his engine."

Carroll's confession, accompanied by a guilty expression, tugged at Kelle's compassionate heart. Stopping outside the infirmary, she patted his arms consolingly. Carroll folded her in his arms for a comforting hug. His need to expunge his guilt, to touch another human being, made Kelle wind her arms around his thick waist loosely.

"It's okay, Carroll. Mike Johnson just has the same virus the others had. It's really not much worse than a very bad cold. You're the one who told me not to let anything as simple as this virus upset me, remember?"

"Umm-hmm," Carroll answered. Putting his forehead against hers, he whispered, "If you need me during the night you know I'll help you any way I can."

Someone clearing his throat made Carroll and Kelle spring apart like guilty teenagers on the front porch when the light is flicked on.

"Well, well. What have we here, Doctor?"

"Ensign Taylor, what we have here is a man worried about a friend who is being comforted by the friend's doctor," Carroll snarled, resenting the implication in the inquirer's voice.

Taylor's disbelief was obvious in his expression. Carroll took two steps toward the young navy ensign.

"Mike is my friend too. Think I can get in on some of this . . . comforting?"

The meaning was unmistakable. Quickly Kelle stepped between the two hostile men. For some reason Taylor was spoiling for a barroom brawl, and Carroll looked more than ready to defend her reputation.

"Don't be ridiculous . . . either of you. I don't have time to patch up split knuckles and black eyes. You both say you're Mike's friends? Prove it. He's the one who needs medical attention. Both of you shake hands, then clear out."

Punching Taylor in the mouth isn't going to remove the sneer from his face, Kelle thought as she watched the two men shake hands. Confident Carroll's reputation as a family man would override any slurs passed around by Taylor, Kelle wordlessly turned and entered the infirmary.

"Sorry, Kelle," she heard Mike croak.

He was lying fully clothed on the bed, arm flung over his forehead and eyes, legs crossed at the ankles. Kelle blanched when she heard his apology. What was he apologizing for? Running outside or what had taken place in the equipment room?

"Are you running a fever?" she asked, not willing to talk about either incident.

"Yeah. I'm burning up." Sweat beaded on his forehead. A dark circle of moisture ringed his shirt beneath his armpits.

"Can you get your clothes off while I get the thermometer?" Kelle turned her back to the bed and briskly walked to the cabinet where she kept her stethoscope, digital thermometer, and blood pressure kit. She asked softly, "Do you need any help?"

Mike grunted negatively. His body ached from the top of his head to the tip of his toes, but he wasn't about to let Kelle touch him. He felt that he might explode with shame if she did. Dumb grease jockey, he berated himself. First you hurt Kelle, then you damage your own health. God damned jerk! Stripped down to his jockey shorts, he slid between the cool crispness of the clean sheets.

Advancing toward the bed, Kelle reassured Mike as she would any patient. "You'll be okay." She placed her hand on his forehead. A thin sheen of perspiration covered his brow. The fiery heat radiating beneath her hand alarmed Kelle. Mike Johnson's illness put Benson's in the skinned-knee category. "Open up."

Keeping his eyes shut, Mike opened his mouth and lifted his tongue. I'll never be okay, he thought miserably. I'll recover from the cold, but I'll never feel all right about what I did to her. How could I be dumb enough to lose my temper like a kid and prove my virility by hurting and manhandling a woman? His mouth shifting the plastic gadget to one side, he once again murmured, "Sorry, Kelle."

Keeping her eyes on the rapidly rising digital numbers, she heard his second apology and knew he referred to his disregard of her medical warning at dinner. "Boys will be boys," she replied stiffly. "Stop talking or I won't get an accurate reading."

Mike groaned, feeling as though she had physically slapped him. He had acted like a frustrated boy, but hearing it from her lips made his guilt more acute. He knew she'd never forgive him regardless of how many times he apologized.

One hundred two point seven, Kelle read. It had already entered the dangerous area. "We're going to have to pull that temperature down." Aspirin. Alcohol bath. Penicillin. Keep him filled with fluids, she thought, listing the treatment by priority.

"Okay, Mike. Any allergies I don't know about?"

His throat hurt too much to answer. Barely shaking his head against the pillow brought shafts of pain from the back of his skull forward. Moisture gathered in the corners of his eyes. His mind drifted toward the dark warm cloud of unconsciousness, but he struggled away from it, cursing himself for causing Kelle more problems.

Alert to his struggle to remain conscious, Kelle hurriedly went to the medicine cabinet and extracted a bottle of pills. Filling a paper cup with water, she asked if he could get the pills down. Again Mike barely raised, then lowered his bearded chin. Kelle gently raised his head with one arm and lifted his head. Obediently Mike opened his mouth and allowed her to place the aspirin on his tongue.

"Thirsty," he muttered, swallowing the pills and emptying the small cup. His eyelids felt as though heavy weights rested on them. He wanted to open them, to thank Kelle, to apologize again, but he couldn't. When his head was back on the pillow he heard Kelle moving back to the cabinet. A vision of her straight posture, her softly rounded hips, her long, shapely legs stayed vivid in his mind. Restlessly he shifted in the bed.

Moments later Kelle drew back the sheet to his waist, exposing his powerful arms and muscular chest. A thick forest of dark hair damply curled on his chest. He appeared to have difficulty breathing. Bad sign, Kelle noted as she began wiping a cloth soaked in alcohol over his chest. Bronchial pneumonia wasn't outside the realm of possibility. His skin felt as though a stoked furnace burned from within.

Kelle dipped the cloth back into the alcohol solution, wrung it out, and repeated the procedure. Carefully she wiped away the beads of perspiration on his forehead. Frustrated by the limited amount of medical care she could administer with the facilities at her disposal, she prayed silently. During their long months of isolation she had never felt this helpless, this alone.

Throughout the night Mike alternated between burning up with fever and jerkily shivering from bouts of chills. Keeping a constant vigil, Kelle kept the blankets covering him, forced him to drink water, fed him aspirin and administered antibiotics. Running on adrenaline and fear, she never rested.

"Kelle?"

"I'm here, Mike," she answered, taking the hand he raised slightly off the olive-drab blanket. His hand was hot . . . dry. "Do you need something?"

"Hot. So damned hot," he complained in a parched whisper.

"I know," she soothed, "I know." Leaning forward, she placed her cool hand on his forehead. Perspiration had dampened his longish hair making it wave.

Until he heard her voice, felt her soothing

touch on his brow, Mike thought he'd died and gone to hell. Only the lowest depths of hell could be this stifling hot. He tried to smile as she lightly squeezed his fingertips, but failed. His parched mouth tasted of half-dissolved aspirin.

"Time?"

"Morning. A bit after seven o'clock."

"You . . . sleep?"

"Off and on," she lied. "Drink some water?"

He nodded his head and realized it didn't hurt as badly as it had, but try as he might, he couldn't open his eyes. Helpless as a babe, he felt water dribble out of the corner of his mouth as he labored to swallow. Disgraceful, he chided, his tongue too thick to apologize for his clumsiness.

Kelle wiped away the trickle and sank back into her chair. The damned fever won't break, she cursed. There ought to be something more I can do. But what? If only they were near a hospital where the proper tests and diagnosis could be made.

Elbows propped on her knees, fingertips covering her lips, she racked her brain for a treatment. There wasn't anything else she could do. Over and over in her mind she compared Benson's symptoms with Mike's. The slight swelling on the sides of Mike's neck, and the smallish lump under his arm, indicated another possibility. If he had what she suspected, the only truly effective treatment was sleep, sleep, and more sleep.

The door opened, drawing her attention away from Mike and her worrisome thoughts. Carroll Kleinschmidt quietly walked into the room carrying a tray.

"How's the patient, Doc?" he asked.

Kelle motioned him out of the room. She hadn't been able to get a throat culture and she wasn't going to expose any of the other team members unnecessarily. Stiff from sitting upright all night, she walked to the door like an old woman.

"No change," she said when they were both outside. Kelle left the door open a crack in case Mike needed her. Glancing back into the room, she positioned herself so she could keep an eye on Mike's still form.

"Shouldn't the fever have broken by now?"

"Not necessarily. Benson's wasn't this high, but it lasted a full twenty-four hours."

"Thank goodness modern medicine has a magical black bag full of medical tricks, huh?"

"I'm not sure, Carroll. It's pretty bad. I'm putting the quarantine sign on the door just in case he's infectious. Would you have someone deliver a tray when they've finished eating? He needs to sleep. Have them knock and leave it outside the door."

"You suspect something other than what Benson had, don't you?"

Kelle shook her head. "I took a blood sample. His white count is up. I think there may be some swelling in the glands along his neck. If we were back home I'd suspect infectious mononucleosis."

"The kissing disease?" Carroll translated.

"That's the layman's term for it."

"But how would he get it down here?"

"Not from kissing anyone. Sometimes people are undiagnosed carriers. Just like a tuberculosis carrier prior to the patch test."

"Terrific. We have Taylor sniggering innuendoes and Mike with the kissing disease. And to round the picture out, everyone will see the quarantine sign on the door and suspect the two of you are having a good old time."

"I stated a medical opinion based on a meager amount of information, Carroll. But regardless of the consequences, I'm not taking any chance of infecting others. I'll enter the diagnosis in the medical log. There's no reason to tell anyone else."

"Okay. You're the doctor."

"You should be relieved. His crazy romp outside wouldn't have affected his blood count one way or another if he has mono."

Carroll grinned. "Thanks. You take care of Mike and I'll check back later."

Back inside the room, Kelle checked his vital signs, recorded them on the chart at the foot of the bed, then resumed her diligent watch. Although his fever remained dangerously high, he appeared to have drifted into a light, restless sleep.

Twelve hours later he began muttering deliriously. Kelle heard her name mingled with those of others. Then he lapsed into a period of unintelligible muttering. The harsh, disjointed whispers lasted for only a few minutes until he drifted back to sleep. Slowly his temperature began dropping a fraction of a degree at a time.

The longer she observed him the more certain she was that the mono diagnosis was incorrect. Whatever was wrong with Mike, getting his temperature down remained all important, Kelle thought. Rolling her head around to relieve the tension that was draining her body of vitality, Kelle winced at the sharp tug on the hairs leading to the long braids coiled on her head.

It was late. Normally in the sanctity of her own room she would have unbraided her hair and thoroughly brushed it by now. She gave a jaw popping yawn and rose from her chair. Kelle took off her shoes and silently paced the width of the room as she began removing the numerous hairpins that held her braids in place. Earlier Carroll had brought her a change of clothing and cosmetic essentials, which she had placed in the cubbyhole bathroom. The waist-length braids, seemingly with a will of their own, began unwinding as she picked up the brush.

Kelle shook the long length of platinum hair loose and lightly massaged her scalp. Too tired to think straight, she washed her hair and brushed her teeth. Her glasses in one hand and brush in the other, she returned to her vigil feeling somewhat refreshed. She'd performed her ritual one hundred strokes when she saw, out of the corner of her eye, Mike's hand raise an inch or so off the bed.

"Thirsty," he barely whispered.

Within seconds she held a cup in one hand and propped up his head into the crook of her arm with the other. She noticed his eyes were open, but somewhat glazed. The fever, regardless of the cause, had taken its toll.

"Better?"

"Better," he repeated.

Kelle twisted at the waist to replace the cup on the bedside cart. Used to her hair being on top of her head, she immediately apologized when she felt his hand tangle in the long length as it brushed against his face.

"Don't be sorry," he objected hoarsely. His large hand held on to her hair when she attempted to move. "Don't."

## CHAPTER FOUR

Half on, half off the bed, Kelle knew her position was becoming increasingly precarious. His pleading tone held her captive. "Let me pull the chair over before I fall on top of you."

"No." He shifted a few inches away from her but refused to let go of her hair. "Please."

"Mike, you're sick. You don't know what you're doing." She felt his large hand raise higher on her back to the base of her neck. He let the sheer strands of her hair slip through his hands.

A sharp shiver coursed through his body, visibly shaking him.

"Chills?" she questioned, bending closer to his face.

"Cold, Kelle. Stone cold."

Kelle flushed, not knowing whether he referred to his own chills or her initial response to his domineering kiss earlier. In either case he didn't need to become upset.

"Let go and I'll get you another blanket," she bargained, refusing to sit on the bed.

Mike flipped back the corner of the covers, retaining his grip on the silver-blond hair threaded between his fingers. "Keep me warm," he begged huskily.

Her blue eyes widening, she searched his face trying to decide if he was aware of what he was doing. Another chill shuddered through him.

"Damn it, Mike." She jerked the cover back up over his bared thigh. "This isn't the time to play games." His hand tightened its hold.

Kelle pulled her hair over her shoulder, but his grip tightened. One by one she began peeling his fingers loose. When his thumb traced the tip of her breast he regained his hold on her hair. Again he pulled the covers down.

"Please."

Once again Kelle hoisted them upward. "Mike Johnson. You let go of my hair . . . immediately."

She thought she'd won when his hand slipped lower, but then he began winding individual locks around each finger, binding his fingers, leaving his thumb free to investigate the puckered nipple encased in lace.

"Fire and ice," he whispered. "So cold. Come to bed." She watched him stiffen his jaw to keep his teeth from chattering. "Please," he begged softly.

She knew she couldn't do it. And yet she couldn't deny the desire to lie beside him, to warm his shivering flesh with her own.

"Oh, Mike. What am I going to do with you?" She sighed, weakening.

"Keep me warm" was his pinch-lipped answer.

Of her own accord she raised the sheet and blankets and slid between them. It didn't matter how close she got to him at this point. She was already more than exposed to whatever virus he had. Immediately Mike drew her close. He shook from the chills. For long minutes he absorbed her fiery warmth, the warmth of her body, the warmth of her heart.

Kelle didn't kid herself into believing she was performing a humanitarian act. Somewhere along the way she had realized that she was deeply attracted to Mike Johnson. He did something to her that no other man ever had. He disturbed her and excited her and she yearned to touch him and feel the crush of his mouth against hers.

She knew they were completely mismatched, but for the moment she didn't care. All she wanted was to lie beside Mike.

Mike knew he was dreaming an impossible dream. A dream he refused to awaken from. The freezing cold that had penetrated him to the bone slowly began to dissipate. The nightmares he had suffered through deliriously the night before were replaced by ecstatic fantasies so real they were believable. He embraced Kelle closer, trying to prevent his dream from fading away.

A cold sweat drenched his forehead as his temperature steadily declined. He could hear Kelle; he didn't answer. To speak would break the magic spell.

Tenderly she stroked his brow. It was cooler than before, but she realized his temperature remained above normal. This explained his exhausted deep sleep.

Careful not to awaken him, she left the perspiration-scented bed. Unable to resist, she ran one last caressing hand over Mike's face and shoulder. The dampness of the bed linen distressed her. A man who had been burning up with fever only hours ago could suffer a relapse easily. With long strides she moved to the linen closet, then swiftly, efficiently she changed the sheets and wiped the dried perspiration off Mike. Only once did he whisper her name, and that was when she had comfortably settled his dark head on the fresh pillowcase.

Exhausted herself, Kelle put the two armchairs together and made a temporary bed.

It was nearly two days later when Mike finally fully regained consciousness. Slowly he opened his eyes to find Kelle dozing in a chair.

He watched her lovingly as she slept and remembered a dream he had had about her. How he wished it had actually happened. At least he could remember the dream clearly. Perhaps it would be as close as he would ever come to having Kelle in bed with him. Mike groaned. Was remembering going to be a blessing? Most likely it would be a torment. Closing his eyes, he tried to re-create the manifestation.

Shame burned his cheeks. *What kind of man am I to have lurid fantasies about the woman who waited on me hand and foot during my illness?* he wondered. Even though it would have served me right if she had pushed my carcass out in the snow for my previous brutality. During the rational moments between the recurring bouts of fever, he remembered apologizing. But he knew she hadn't believed his sincerity.

Mike heard a soft stirring beside the bed. Eyes open, he rolled on his side and watched her slowly awaken. Her blue eyes shone softly in the near darkness.

"Kelle, I'm sorry. I didn't mean for it to happen. I'm truly sorry I manhandled you." Mike forced the words out quickly. He hoped to impress her with his abject apology the first thing, before she remembered what a cad he had been.

"Sorry?" Kelle mumbled, her brain still foggy from sleep. "You're sorry?"

"Yes, I am. I'd give anything for it not to have happened. I don't know what came over me. Can I convince you I would never force myself on an unwilling woman?"

Kelle braced her forearm against the chair and raised into an upright position. "I was willing," she replied truthfully.

"Don't try to make me feel better. You resisted; I forced you."

Kelle grinned. "I'll accept an apology for the harsh kiss over in the equipment room, but nothing else."

"Nothing else?" Oh, God. I must have talked in my sleep, Mike thought, anguished. Mike rubbed his hand over his beard and felt the soreness from having gritted his teeth to keep any mutterings to himself. "The dream. I won't excuse my sexual ramblings by saying I had a fever—"

Kelle interrupted, "Dream? Which dream?"

"I won't embarrass you further by talking about it," Mike answered, wanting to hide his head beneath the pillow.

"Must have been some dream," Kelle teased as she swept off the covers and approached the bed.

"It was. Teenage boys have sexual fantasies like that, not grown men."

"Where's the cocky, arrogant man who threatened to give me biology lessons?" she continued. "Wish I could remember and be forced to apologize for *my* dreams."

Even now Kelle's presence affected Mike as strongly as the gale winds the South Pole was famous for. How was he going to make it through the days and nights ensconced in the infirmary with Kelle moving about in her quiet way, taking care of him?

"My fever's down, isn't it?" he asked, driving his thoughts away from the soft touch of her fingertips as she held the sensitive inner side of his thick wrist. "I should be able to go back to duty after breakfast, right?"

"Who's the doctor here? Me or you?"

"You're the doctor, but I'm the diesel mechanic who needs to keep a close check on the equipment."

"Not today you're not. In fact, probably not for the remainder of the week."

"You're going to keep me in here for five days . . . and nights?"

"Scared?" she asked, laughing at the expression of horror on his face.

He coughed. "Spitless."

Kelle took the thermometer out of its holder and stuck it under his tongue. "Don't worry, Mike. I haven't lost a patient yet."

"Was it really just a dream?" he blurted when she removed the instrument. It had seemed so very real, he couldn't feel sure but had to know. He remembered twining his hands into her hair, watching her climbing between the sheets, drawing her close to his freezing body. But after those recollections, the memories became confused, less focused.

Kelle saw his face contorting, preparing for another apology. "Nothing happened, Mike. You didn't use your illness to gain sympathy or to seduce the doctor. For Pete's sake, don't apologize again!"

"Lady, I can't stay here. I'll go stark raving crazy," he whispered in a hoarse voice.

Intentionally misinterpreting his statement, Kelle chuckled. "Difficult patients are my specialty. I promise—you won't be bored."

Although weak, Mike wanted to groan in frustration. He wasn't worried about being bored. During the night he had dreamed of a hundred and one different ways Kelle could entertain him. But not one of them could be voiced to a respectable woman.

"I despise being tended to like a helpless kitten," he responded. Let her think my male ego won't survive having her cater to me. Any excuse for getting out of here is better than the real reason.

"Take a deep breath," she instructed as she placed the stethoscope beside his dark, flat nipple. "Again," she ordered, moving the instrument to another position.

She could hear the steady rhythm of his heartbeat, but she also heard fluid in his lungs. Mike Johnson wasn't going anywhere for quite a while. He could scream and yell his protests, but a man with pneumonia wasn't getting out of bed.

"You'll be lucky to get out of here in five days," she said quietly. "Where do you want your shot?"

"Shot?"

"As in needle, syringe—antibiotics." Kelle straightened and removed the stethoscope from her ears.

"Now hear this," Mike replied, picking up the listening device and speaking directly into it, enunciating each word precisely. "I am putting my clothes on and getting out of here."

Kelle shook her head and moved backward. "I should let you try. You couldn't get your pants on, much less walk out of here." When Mike flipped the covers back, determination written on his face, she gave him a quick shove before he could sit up in bed. "Don't let stubbornness overload your judgment. You're under doctor's care and doctor's orders. I order you to stay in bed and roll over."

"You remind me of a marine drill sergeant I had in boot camp," Mike sputtered. The effort it had taken to raise his shoulders off the pillow left his head swirling. And yet he felt compelled to either get out or put some kind of barrier between them.

"A patient isn't allowed to insult his doctor. Don't you know the first rule regarding hospitalization?"

"No," he answered shortly. "What is the first rule regarding hospitalization?"

Approaching the medicine cabinet for the small bottle of antibiotic, she smiled. "Use a fishhook needle for uncooperative patients."

"Ouch." Mike groaned, smiling himself. "You wouldn't do that to a poor, sick, defenseless patient, would you?"

"Umm-hmm." Once the syringe was filled, she returned to the side of the bed. "Roll over and pull down your shorts," she teased. "And don't worry, I'll still respect you in the morning."

She listened to him chuckle at her words.

Mike barely felt the sting of the alcohol or the prick of the short needle.

"Will you?" he asked when he rolled back over.

"Sure I will. That's part of the Hypocritical Oath," she answered.

"You mean Hypocr—" He stopped himself midword. "You shouldn't joke about being a doctor. It's a serious profession. People look up to doctors."

Laughing aloud, Kelle offered Mike a drink of water before getting the tray of food set by the door.

"We practice medicine. If we had everything right we wouldn't have to practice, would we?"

"You don't take yourself too seriously, do you?"

Kelle motioned for him to sit up, then propped the tray over his legs. "I take my work seriously, but not the holier-than-thou attitude many doctors feel they earned when they received their M.D. diploma."

Stomach growling, Mike picked up the fork and uncovered the dish, anticipating a full ration of meat, potatoes, and bread. Instead, a bowl of creamed something-or-other stared him in the face.

"This is supposed to make me well? I can't

eat mush for dinner. I'll starve to death!" he protested.

"Don't quibble or I'll hook the I.V. up again," Kelle threatened with mock sternness.

A teasing light entered Mike's eyes. "You'll have to feed me. I'm too weak." He held his hand straight out and let it tremble.

"You're faking, aren't you?"

Shaking his shaggy head, Mike denied the accusation. Perhaps the best way to get out of the infirmary was to be too agreeable.

"I wouldn't want you to have to clean up the mess I'd make feeding myself." His jaw dropped expectantly.

Kelle pulled up a chair to the bed. Spoon in hand, she filled it, then lightly shoved it into his waiting mouth. He grimaced at the bland flavor, swallowed, and waited for another bite. His gaze never left her face.

Had he really considered her plain when he had first seen her? he asked himself, unable to believe his own shallow impression. How had she managed to change his first reaction so drastically? She might not be beautiful, but she certainly was pretty. Perhaps he hadn't seen the inner glow she radiated. Or perhaps the formal, mannish handshake she had bestowed on him had been offputting. How different she is, he mused, from the image she tries so hard to project.

Kelle devoted her entire concentration to getting the spoon from the bowl to his mouth without drowning him in porridge. His intent stare rattled her. She kept her eyes on the spoon. This meal would be the first and last she would spend hand-feeding him, she promised herself.

"Enough," Mike mumbled, his mouth feeling as though a jar of white, liquid glue had been shoved into it. "My mother used to say, 'Eat it; it will stick to your ribs.' Now I know what she meant." His hand rubbed over the thick patch of hair on his chest.

He watched Kelle carefully pick up the tray and place it outside the door. Several days isolated with Kelle would be difficult for him to endure. The attraction he felt was too strong. To spend each night dreaming about her while she was within touching distance asked too much of his self-control.

Unknown to Mike, Kelle's thoughts were traveling down the same path. His being weak and helpless touched her caring nature. She had lain in his bed, felt his feverish warmth, nursed him through the critical first stages of his illness. She couldn't ignore the effect his penetrating eyes had on her. Nor could she dismiss the joy she experienced when she heard him laugh, heard him talk to her in his low, husky voice. But what could she do?

She couldn't kick a sick man out of the infirmary. He'd be out messing around with those engines faster than the wind blew the snow. Complications could easily set in. But if he stayed there with her, there were certainly other complications to worry about. Which complication was the lesser of two evils?

Her train of thought was broken by Mike calling her name. Keep up the doctor-patient routine, she instructed herself silently as she pivoted.

"Bed bath or tub bath?" she inquired.

"You aren't going to bathe me, are you?" Mike demanded, diverted from what he originally intended to say.

Kelle looked around the room. "Do you see anyone else here to do it?"

"Oh, no, you don't. I'm perfectly capable of washing my own hide."

"Who do you think has been washing it for the past three days?" she inquired, lips quirking upward at his modest grasping of the sheet up to his neck. "Besides, patients who, by their own admission, can't feed themselves obviously can't be expected to bathe themselves," she said with a wicked grin.

"No wonder I smell like a gorilla dipped in alcohol on a South African slave ship," he muttered. "Don't worry, I can wash myself."

He gritted his teeth, swung his long legs

from beneath the sheets, stiffened his weak knees. Head spinning, he navigated a weaving course into the bathroom. Confident he'd feel better after taking a bath, he steadied himself against the cool wall and bent over to turn the faucet on.

"I'll get it," he heard from the doorway. "And they talk about liberated women being muleheaded," she berated. "We certainly have strong images to emulate."

In the confined space, their bodies unavoidably brushing against each other, Mike groaned in frustration.

"Are you worse?" Kelle anxiously inquired. "Put your arm around my shoulder and I'll take you back to bed."

"Kelle, for God's sake, get out of here. I can manage," he barked hoarsely. "You're going to have a basket case if you keep brushing against me that way."

Shocked at his admission, Kelle backed out of the small room. Mike shoved the door shut in her face, but it didn't break the tension between the two of them. Much as Kelle wanted to she couldn't turn back the hands of time and eliminate the kisses they had shared. She couldn't black out the feelings she had for Mike. She loved Mike Johnson; she wanted him. They were two adults, isolated beyond the isolation of the South Pole.

By the time Mike had completed bathing, Kelle had unbound the tight braids from the top of her head and slipped into her striped pajamas. It was late and she was exhausted. The cat naps she had taken when caring for Mike had barely been enough to keep her going.

Separated from her by less than six feet, Mike stood in the doorway, frozen in place. Feeling one hundred percent better after his soaking, he wondered if he was hallucinating.

"Kelle?" he whispered, wondering if his eyes were deceiving him. Mentally he tried to remember if she had been sleeping in street clothes on the previous nights when he had awoken, or if she had been wearing what she had on now.

"Mike?" she replied, looking at the turned-back bed.

Seconds silently slipped past them, unretrievable, wasted. "Are you certain?" he whispered.

Mutely she nodded her head, unable to voice her invitation to share his bed.

"Last night I dreamed about you. Afraid I'd wake up I clenched my jaw shut to keep from saying the words of love I need to say now. I love you, Kelle."

She smiled serenely. "It's crazy, but I came to the same conclusion several days ago."

"You're like a fantasy come true for me."

Kelle felt at ease with Mike. Somehow she knew she'd be able to express her secret fears and joys, say things, do things she would have been too inhibited to do with anyone else.

"Come to bed," Kelle said softly. "You'll have to tell me about your fantasies."

Mike crossed the small room and sank on the opposite side of the bed. He interlaced his fingers behind his head, watching her. "In my dreams . . ." he swallowed deeply. "You unbutton your shirt first."

One button at a time, spreading the cotton fabric as she went, Kelle followed his direction until her pajama top hung loosely open. Kelle watched his eyes cling to the inches of bare skin and cleavage exposed.

Kelle removed the top, pausing before tossing it on the nearby chairs she had previously slept in.

"Talk to me, Mike. Women have fantasies too."

"Your breasts are beautiful. White mounds tipped with golden-brown nipples. My God, Kelle, I can remember the sweet taste of them in my dream." He sat up. He examined his hands, then let them fall palm upward on the sheet. "The bottoms?" he croaked.

With a quick motion she began lowering them. She wiggled her hips to shrug out of them just as Mike's muscular leg came out from beneath the sheet. She watched his foot touch the floor as though he could no longer tolerate the languid pace.

"Don't get up."

"Honey"—he sighed with exasperation—"I don't know if I'm dizzy from anticipation or from having spent three days in bed."

Concern wiped the slight, sensuous smile from her face. "Maybe you haven't recovered enough for this."

"Kelle, if you stop now I swear I'll go in the bathroom and cut my wrists!"

Laughing at his threat, Kelle hooked her thumb in the elastic waistband and casually threw her pajama bottoms on the chair.

Her clothes removed, she edged toward him. Provocatively she cupped her breasts, then lightly ran her palms over the indentation of her waist, the flair of her hips.

Mike whispered, "Still feeling daring, I see."

Kelle smoothed her hands over the wide expanse of his shoulders and chest as Mike drew her forward and nuzzled her breasts. For long moments his hands slowly explored the secret hollows and crevices with gentle strokes.

When Mike drew her full length against his muscular body, demanding her lips, Kelle shuddered. She delighted in the feel of his heart pounding against her own.

"Touch me, Kelle. I'm yours," he said, his voice hoarse with passion.

Bold as she had been while undressing, her fingers shook as she traced the V of hair on his chest. As her hand tentatively moved lower, Mike trembled, then bent, seeking the sensitive tips of her breasts.

Arousing this strong man made Kelle feel a power she'd never experienced. Although he throbbed with strength, his body trembled with a weakness only she could end.

She heard the same plea he'd made in his dreams other nights: "Take me . . . God, take me!" Mike growled the words as he forced them into her mouth with a passionate kiss.

His strong hands raised her hips. No longer able to restrain his hunger, he entered her with one swift stroke. Afraid he might have hurt her, he broke the kiss and looked at her face. There wasn't any pain to be seen, only a slight smile and wide sparkling eyes.

"You're wonderful, love," he cooed. "I'd like to stay like this, for all eternity."

Kelle peppered kisses across his bearded face. "Love me," she moaned.

Laughing triumphantly at her willingness, Mike thrust deeply. "Next time will be slower, for both of us."

Together they shared the physical glory of their loving union. Mike repeated her name over and over, telling her how much he loved her. He gave her all the words, the kisses, he could no longer contain. This was no dream. This was heaven on earth.

Later, satiated, they lay entwined. Neither of them heard or saw the door open and the empty tray being removed from the room.

For an instant a pair of eyes watched Kelle stroke the length of Mike's shoulder, waist, and hip in her sleep. She was a woman, the only woman, and he wanted her. Confident of himself as a lover, he knew he could have her screaming with delight. If she would bed a diesel mechanic she'd probably die of ecstasy in his arms.

But not now. I'll take her later, once Mike Johnson is out of the way, he thought as he backed out of the door. He'd have her. If he was generous they'd probably all have her before the next few weeks were over.

As silently as he opened the door, he closed it.

## CHAPTER FIVE

During the remaining days of Mike's stay in the infirmary, Kelle divided her work between finalizing the data necessary for her special report and taking care of him. Mike Johnson abhorred being idle. Her entire repertoire of card games, word games, and hand-held computer games had been sorely tested as she tried to occupy his days.

The hours the majority of the crew slept, Kelle joined Mike in the infirmary. Their nights, when there was little danger of being interrupted, were spent talking, and loving, and discovering more and more about each other. Kelle felt completely relaxed with him. They discussed their childhoods and teenage years, and Kelle found herself confiding things in Mike that she had never before told anyone.

Kelle hummed a jaunty ditty as she carried Mike's lunch tray back to the dining area. When one of the navy men brushed by her in the corridor she mentally reprimanded him for taking up more than his share of the hallway. The incident reminded her of the early days of the expedition when several men had tested her determination to be aloof. But she had dealt with that problem long ago.

"Hey, Doc," the kitchen helper greeted her, taking the tray out of her hands. "We haven't seen much of you lately. How's Johnson?"

"On the mend," she replied. "He can have the regular menu tonight."

"Took Johnson longer to recover than the others. Guess the Three Hundred Club initiation took it out of him. Too bad you didn't join us. That would have made the run into below-zero temperatures worthwhile." His eyes raked over her and he smiled knowingly.

Automatically Kelle raised her hand and closed the top button of her loose shirt. A frown wrinkled her brow. What had he meant by that? she wondered. Perhaps her overactive imagination was making her sensitive to any masculine attention.

She strode to the door and forced herself to laugh. "You'll have something to brag about when you get home," she quipped.

Coincidence? she questioned once alone in

the hallway headed toward the infirmary. "Guilt," she muttered to herself.

A scarlet letter wasn't tattooed on her forehead. No one could possibly know what she and Mike had been doing. Steps slowing, she allowed time to ponder the men's reaction. Could they suspect more than she thought?

No, it couldn't be. Again she thought it was her own feeling of guilt.

Guilty of what? Having a secret, intimate relationship with another member of the team, she answered honestly. But what choice do we have? This isn't something to post on the recreation room bulletin board. Mentally she pictured tacking a memorandum to the corkboard. To Whom It May Concern: Kelle Langdon is in love. Comments and innuendoes should be in written form and delivered to the infirmary.

In this case, what wasn't known didn't hurt anybody, Kelle decided. She changed her scowl into a smile as she entered the infirmary and greeted Mike.

"I've had a steady stream of visitors today. No objections from the lady doctor, are there?" Mike inquired. He patted the side of the bed. "How about a quick kiss, Kelle? I've missed you."

"With the company you've had?" She listened for sounds in the corridor before moving to the side of the bed and placing a soft kiss on his smiling lips. "At least they've kept your mind occupied."

"Kissing involves my mind and my body. Exercise for the soul," he teased.

"Did any of your visitors make inquiries about your mind, body, or soul?"

"Just the usual good-natured kidding." When she stepped back several paces, eyebrows raised in question, he playfully swatted at her rear end, but missed. "What are you worried about?"

Kelle collapsed into the chair by the bed and pushed a loose hairpin back in place. "The effect our relationship would have on the other men should anyone find out."

"I'm not prone to bragging. You haven't been gossiping, have you?" he joked, not taking the situation seriously.

"Suppose"—she leaned forward earnestly—"suppose you found out I was having an affair with a member of the expedition. How would you feel?"

"I'd feel fine after I dropped him into the nearest crevasse," Mike replied, but he was unable to keep a straight face.

"Not funny. Seriously, what would you think?"

"I think your imagination is running away

with you. Has anyone said or done anything unusual?"

"Maybe. Maybe not. But . . ."

"Doesn't sound like your typical scientific answer," Mike retorted. "Don't create problems that don't exist. What happens between us is behind closed doors. Has anyone ever entered without knocking?"

"No, but . . ."

"Forget it then." Mike leaned over and stroked her hand from wrist to fingertip. "How about a wild game of five-card draw? You better expend your energies trying to win back the thousands you've lost."

"Books of matches are in plentiful supply once we return stateside," she replied with a cheeky grin. "I suspect you've marked the deck while I've been working."

"I warned you at the bridge table that I'm lucky."

"Lucky at cards; unlucky in love," she murmured before thinking.

"That, my dear, is the rationale of a person who loses constantly at cards. I'm lucky . . . period," he stated firmly. "You get the cards and I'll let you deal."

The apprehensive mood lightened as they kidded back and forth, but the anxiety returned once she had left his side.

When Kelle walked into the lounge a while

later, she immediately knew something was wrong. There had been lively conversation wafting down the corridor only moments ago, but the second she entered the room cold silence greeted her. Seven pairs of eyes scrutinized her intently as she stood in the doorway.

"How's the dart tournament going?" she asked, trying to sound more casual than she felt.

"Schwartz is ready to challenge you for championship," Ensign Taylor replied. His lips quirked into a half grin. "Think you can beat him?"

"Easily," Kelle said, striding to the corkboard target to remove the six darts, three red, three blue. The men chuckled as they formed a semicircle beside and behind the twenty-foot line.

At one time or another they had all participated in the game. A running tally of winners and losers stayed posted on the bulletin board nearby. Kelle had always been one of the top contenders or the champ. There was nothing unusual in being challenged to defend her title. But somehow she knew something was amiss.

"Red or blue, Schwartz?"

"Red suits you; I'll take the blue."

Several men snickered, then hid their sniggers with their hands.

"Something going on I should know about?" Kelle asked, becoming suspicious again. To break the monotony, some of the men specialized in pranks. Perhaps the red darts had been rigged not to fly true.

"Nothing you won't find out about in short order," Taylor answered with a sly grin toward the other men.

Kelle shrugged. Most of the time they pulled their practical jokes on each other and left her out. This time, she thought, I'm going to be the butt of one of their pranks.

"Go ahead, Kelle. Ladies first," Schwartz offered with a gallant bow and a flourish of his arm.

Left toe on the line, she placed one dart between thumb and first two fingers, letting her little finger balance her hand. Shoulders straight, she drew her right arm back, then propelled the dart forward, watching with glee as it hit the center of the bull's-eye. She stepped aside with an ear-to-ear grin.

"Not bad for a beginner, huh?"

"Something tells me you're more experienced than any of us guessed," Schwartz replied. His eyes never left the space between the first and second button of her woolen shirt while he spoke. "You played this game stateside, didn't you?"

Innocent of the underlying meaning behind

the question, Kelle answered honestly, "No, but I've practiced for hours since I arrived."

Rowdy laughter echoed through the room. What's so damned funny? Kelle wondered. Why are they staring at me? When she followed the path of one set of smoldering brown eyes, she realized they were staring directly at her breasts. What's going on?

"Practice makes perfect," she heard from one of the support staff. "How's Johnson?"

The two unrelated topics, joined together, fell into place. Somehow the entire crew knew or at least assumed she'd spent the night in Mike's bed. Their eyes, boring into her breasts, the juncture of her thighs, the roundness of her buttocks, were mute testimony to their knowledge. They were hungry and she was the feast.

Horrified at the realization, she could feel the blood draining from her face. How had they found out? Ensign Taylor had seen her hug Carroll, but certainly a platonic exchange hadn't aroused this furor. Had someone come in the room while they slept?

A tiny tremor shook the hand holding the darts.

"I think I've been running a little temperature," Schwartz said before she could answer the inquiry about Mike. "Maybe I'm getting what Mike has. What's the treatment, Doc?"

Anger flooded through her. She pointed the

needle-sharp dart at his stomach and answered in a voice colder than the Antarctic, "In your case, a stroll through a whiteout, Mr. Schwartz, or an increased amount of white powder in your mashed potatoes. Either will bring your temperature down."

Blue eyes blazing, she stared directly into the shocked faces of the other men. "Anyone else feeling bad?"

No one answered. To Kelle's profound relief, none of them moved closer. She had done the unexpected . . . defied their knowledge.

"Well, *gentlemen,* I'm feeling nauseated. I'm certain you'll understand why I'm forfeiting this game." With a wild fling, she threw the darts toward the board and was out of the room before they bounced off the wall and clattered to the ground.

Tears of rage blinded her eyes as she ran through the tunnels heading back to the infirmary. Mentally she called the spectators of the dart game every foul name she could think of. Someone had managed to incite the group, but who? Verbally attacking them had temporarily put them off, but how long would that last? An hour? A day? A week? A shiver of fear ran down her spine.

Kelle wiped her eyes with the back of her hands outside of the clinic door. Should she tell Mike? She shook her head vehemently. In his weakened condition what could she expect him to do? Intimidate them? Beat the hell out of them? Again she shook her head.

The thought of Mike having to physically defend her was repugnant. No one had ever fought battles for her in the past, and just because she'd spent the night with Mike, she couldn't expect him to become her protector. No way. She'd do what she'd always done: take care of the problem herself.

When she entered the room Mike was out of bed, struggling to balance himself and get into his jeans. A pasty-faced Carroll Kleinschmidt stood beside him.

"Get back in that bed, Mike Johnson," she ordered briskly. Hands on her hips, she dared him to disobey the command.

Carroll rushed over. "Kelle. Thank God you're back. I've told Mike about the rumors being spread. The men are acting crazy."

"So I found out. Sit down, Carroll. Mike, I mean it. Get back in bed. There's no reason to get so excited. We'll be able to handle whatever happens," she said, trying to sound more sure than she felt.

Ignoring the command, Mike continued to struggle getting his right leg into his jeans. Kelle crossed the room and pushed hard against his chest. Immediately losing the fragile hold he had on his balance, he fell backward.

"I'll get their minds out of the gutter," Mike huffed as he straightened and swung his legs back off the bed.

"You can't settle this with your fists, especially in the condition you're in now. I've just demonstrated that."

"You caught me off guard."

Kelle settled her hand on his shoulder. "Just lie down again and rest. Violence isn't going to make things any better."

"She's right, Mike," Carroll agreed. He sank back into the chair, a bewildered expression on his face. "God, I can't believe this is happening. Two thirds of those men out there profess to be happily married. What happened to them?"

"There can only be one reason for what they're doing. My guess is someone sneaked in here and saw Mike and me in bed." Kelle couldn't keep a blush from coloring her cheeks. She wasn't ashamed of loving Mike, but the thought of having a voyeur standing in a dark corner bothered the hell out of her.

"Well, there's no doubt in my mind who it was. He's had his eye on you for a long time, Kelle," Carroll said.

"Who?" Mike demanded, his face twisted with anger.

"Schwartz. He's convinced that his wife is

playing around while he's down here. He hasn't received any kind of message from home for weeks and he said it was driving him crazy."

"What are we going to do about this situation?" Kelle asked in a bleak voice.

Mike removed Kelle's restraining hand and shifted his legs to give her room to sit down. "First off, I think Kelle should be restricted to quarters. Then I'll go to the director and inform him of the problem. Is there any way to get her out of here?"

"Maybe in a week or so they'll be able to get a helicopter out of the Mc Murdo base on the coast. Depends on the winds, the cold. But you're right about Ivan. He needs to know." Carroll began rising to his feet.

"Now wait a minute," Kelle protested. "You two act as though I've left the room. This concerns me more than anyone else and I'm not going to let you two make all the decisions." A strong arm looped over her shoulder and pressed her against a massive chest.

"Sorry, love. We were trying to make certain you'll be all right." Mike's words were soft and conciliatory.

"Ivan Svensky isn't going to allow the project to fall apart," Kelle said, placing her hand over the one Mike had on her arm. "The last thing I wanted to happen is this! Don't you dare apologize or tell me it's your fault. I made the choice."

"With a little prompting?" Mike grinned for the first time since she had entered the room.

"Maybe . . . a little," she answered with a chuckle.

"I'm going to have a chat with Ivan. Mike, Kelle, I'm ashamed of my teammates involved in this. What happens between the two of you is your own private business." Carroll rose and walked toward the door. "Just as a precaution, put a chair under the door handle after I leave. I'll identify myself when I get back."

Kelle followed him to the door. "Thanks, Carroll, for being a true friend when times are difficult."

"I'll get back as soon as I can." Carroll patted the side of her face, then closed the door. Kelle dragged one of the chairs over and lodged it beneath the door handle.

She heard a heavy sigh as she turned around. Mike's shoulders were slumped forward, his chin resting on his chest. Raising his head, his eyes pierced and probed past her glasses. "This is a hellava mess I've gotten you into. I'm sorry you're in this precarious situation."

"And I'm sorry. But I'm not sorry about . . . us." Kelle stepped to the end of the bed. "Are you?"

"Never. I'd like to take your glasses, along

with your clothes, and lock them away for the duration." Mike opened his arms, inviting her to step into them. As they settled around her shoulders, he whispered, "But I'm not going to. For your safety, once I leave this room, I'm not going to touch you again until we're both home." The low groan from deep in his throat told her how difficult keeping this vow was going to be.

Her nose nuzzled against the side of his neck, against his soft beard, Kelle wanted to groan herself. Mike had brought her into a world of sensuality that she had almost forgotten existed and she yearned to investigate it further. But she knew that to do so while stationed here would be sheer folly, madness. Ivan would be able to control the men so long as she and Mike cooperated by not flaunting their affair. To do otherwise would be courting disaster.

Mike kissed her gently on her forehead. "Kelle, Kelle, Kelle," he whispered.

He found himself in a dilemma of his own making. He wanted Kelle. He loved Kelle. But inwardly he wondered if their love could survive anywhere but in their isolated surroundings. He was certain that anything Kelle felt for him would dissolve under the heat of the Texas sun. She could be physically attracted to a man like him, but he was sure that nothing permanent could ever evolve.

"Mike, is your throat still sore?" Kelle asked when she heard him swallow raggedly.

"No, love," *only my heart.*

Kelle moved toward him intent upon checking for any glandular swelling. When she looked directly into his brown-rimmed, blue eyes, she thought she saw a shimmer of moisture, but then he blinked and it was gone. "Let me have a look."

"No, it's not necessary."

"Mike, don't be difficult. No matter what our relationship might develop into, I'm still responsible for your health as long as we stay here. Now, lift your arms."

Once again she discovered no swollen glands. She stood, ready to whip back the sheet.

"Doctor . . . take my word for it. My glands aren't swollen down there either." His fingertips clutched the sheet up below his chin.

"You aren't going to be bashful now, are you? Let go of the sheet!"

"No!" Mike whispered hoarsely. "This reminds me of a game I played as a child with the little girl next door."

"I gather you were always the doctor?"

"As a matter of fact I was," Mike answered with a wide, toothy grin. "But I made such a lasting professional impression on her, she grew up to be a doctor herself."

"So much for chauvinism in the eighties. Drop the sheet, Johnson," she commanded in a pseudo-stern voice.

He clamped the sheet beneath his armpits and lunged forward, grabbing her around the waist. Briefly, explicitly he told her why she wasn't going to go poking around down there. Kelle couldn't keep back a girlish giggle. When he released her she straightened back up. "Mr. Johnson, you're impossible."

"Dr. Langdon, the situation is impossible. Believe me, my reaction will be predictable."

Kelle lifted the chart off the end of the bed and momentarily studied it. "Just wait until Washington reads what I'm writing on your chart," she teased, making imaginary swirls with her pen. "This will teach you to be disrespectful."

Mike grabbed the clipboard. The checks and squiggles had little meaning. "Doctors need penmanship classes."

Kelle laughed at the common layman complaint. "It adds to the mystique. Give me the chart back."

"Not until you tell me what you're going to write."

Kelle rolled her laughing eyes toward the

ceiling. "How about a small heart with your initials on top of mine?"

"Good diagnosis, Doc." He handed the chart back to her.

"It's one Washington would certainly take note of. What do I put down here?" she wondered aloud. "I can't in all honesty determine why you had such a high fever. If you and Benson shared the same germs, you'd be hacking away right now. The culture I took doesn't show anything either."

"Does it matter?"

"Everything that happens down here matters. We're the forerunners of the space laboratories of the future."

"And you'd like to be there too, wouldn't you?"

Laughing at the wistfulness she heard in his own voice, she replied, "Wouldn't you?"

"Yeah, but your chances of getting there are better than mine," he replied seriously.

A sharp rap at the door, followed by Carroll's voice, broke into their sharing of future dreams.

Ivan and Carroll entered the room one behind the other.

"I've called a general meeting of the staff. You three are to stay here until my colleagues straighten themselves out." Ivan turned toward Kelle. "Don't act defensive around the men. Neither of you has done anything wrong. You're to report directly to me should there be any problems with any of the personnel."

"Yes, sir," Kelle answered.

Ivan never beat around the bush. His job required decisiveness. Problems were to be dealt with as rapidly as humanly possible. Hesitating at the wrong time could mean disaster for the expedition, and Ivan was determined not to let that happen.

"Johnson? How are you feeling?" the director demanded as he edged closer to the bed.

"Well enough to resume my duties," Mike replied in a clipped voice.

"That's my decision," Kelle objected.

"Fine, Dr. Langdon," Ivan agreed, shaking his balding gray head. "Carroll is staying here to allay gossip. No reflection on the two of you. What happened in the lounge was inexcusable. Any man who gets out of line will be under immediate house arrest."

"Thank you, Dr. Svensky," Mike said, always a bit awed by the man's presence.

"No thanks necessary, young man. You're both consenting adults. What happens between the two of you is your business and no one else's. I'll see to that. We'll be out of here soon. I don't want any blot on the record."

Ivan shoved the chair away from the door and departed.

"Wheeeew!" Carroll gasped. "The old man is livid. Heads are going to roll at that meeting."

Two days later, Mike left the infirmary. During that time, the men were cordial toward Kelle. Whatever Ivan had said or done was effective. To Kelle's great relief, the matter seemed to disappear as though suspended in outer space.

When she was alone in her room at night, ready for bed, she found herself staring at the ceiling conjuring up a mental picture of Mike. Hollywood should have a talent scout here at the Pole, she thought. But I've fallen in love with more than Mike's handsome face and well-built body, Kelle admitted to herself. She rolled to her side, back to the door, and curled into a tight ball.

They had so little time together. In less than two weeks, weather permitting, they would begin breaking camp. And what would happen then? the level-headed practical side of her nature asked. What will happen when they arrive in New Zealand and Mike is suddenly confronted with more beautiful women than he can handle? Kelle was uncertain she could hold his interest.

In the dark silence she suddenly heard the latch on her door click. Fear lodged in her throat.

"Who's out there?" she called as she threw back the covers and quickly climbed out of the bed.

No answer.

Slipping into the bathrobe she'd draped on the end of the bed, she hesitated momentarily, then crossed the room and flung the door open. Kelle looked to the left, then to the right. Was she hearing things? She started to turn back into her room when another noise, one caused by the terrycloth robe flaring as she turned, drew her attention to the floor. She stooped and picked up a small flat dish filled with black, charred ashes.

Thoughtfully she once again looked both ways down the empty corridor, then closed her door, the dish still in her hand. With the light from the hallway no longer providing light, she was literally and figuratively in the dark. Her hand reached to the side of the door jamb and flicked the lights on.

"What does it mean?" she muttered, perplexed. "Someone leaves a bowl filled with ashes outside my door?"

Is someone threatening to burn the station down? she thought wildly. The smell of the burned paper filled her with fear. Within minutes the entire station could be ablaze, and there was little water to extinguish a fire.

Should I alert Ivan?

Flicking on the overhead light, she used her finger to sort through the ashes. At the bottom of the shallow dish was a corner of paper with tiny block letter written on it.

A shiver of fear ran up her spine as she read the words aloud in a horrified voice: "BURN WITH ME!"

## CHAPTER SIX

Kelle's hand covered her mouth as she gasped. There could be no misconstruing the message. Ivan's lecture obviously hadn't had the desired effect. It had merely changed overt advances into covert threats. She shivered. Was it Schwartz? Taylor? Or could it be someone none of them suspected? Suddenly all the men on the team seemed dangerous and threatening.

Seldom had Kelle known fear, but now it enveloped her with the blinding impact of a polar storm. She felt helpless against its force. Her hand shook as she knocked the tiny scrap of paper off her forefinger with her thumb, returning it to its black bed of ashes.

She put the dish on the built-in desk and

nervously glanced back at the door. There was no lock. She had no weapon to defend herself with. Anyone who wanted to could come in. Where is he now? she wondered. He could be silently waiting down the hallway. Anytime during the remaining days he could catch her alone. . . . Her imagination swirled around in a frightening maze.

Kelle heard a loud roaring in her ears and a spasm of dizziness swept over her. No time to faint, she admonished. She sank to the floor and thrust her head between her knees.

Get out of here. Get out of here, she repeated to herself. But where could she go? Kelle inhaled deeply, realizing that the man who had left the note could be anywhere.

"Oh, Mike, where are you when I need you?"

The sound of her own voice somehow shocked Kelle back to reality, and anger began replacing fear. Her hand clenched into an angry fist. No man would find her cowering on the floor of her bedroom. Physical violence was abhorrent to her, but she could defend herself if necessary.

The man evidently was a coward. Clambering to her feet, she reexamined the contents of the dish. She began trying to figure out her tormentor's personality. He hadn't opened the door and entered; he'd skulked away. The block lettering on the scrap of paper ensured his anonymity. Perhaps his fear of discovery is as great as my fear of attack, she thought.

Kelle went to her clothes chest and removed a six-celled flashlight. It would afford two things: a source of light in the darkened corridor and a weapon of sorts. She pushed the on button, checking to make certain it worked. A beam of light danced across the wall. She turned it off and hurriedly pulled clean clothing out of the drawers. Eyes on the door, remaining close to the flashlight, she shed her nightclothes and donned her work apparel.

Quickly she quelled the urge to run to Mike. He would discourage any man from tangling with her while under his protective wing. He'd come to her aid, she didn't doubt that, but his method of finding the culprit would be to string every man up by his thumbs until one of them admitted to the charred offering. The tiny, scratchlike scars on his knuckles were all the indication she needed as to what method he'd choose to solve this kind of problem.

Much as she wanted to have his strong arms wrap around her protectively, she would follow the chain of command. Ivan, known for his late work habits, would probably still be in his office. Kelle opened the top drawer, dumped out the cosmetics contained in a small plastic bag, and placed the contents of the bowl inside the sack. She wasn't about to travel down the empty corridors letting the evidence blow out of the dish.

The door squeaked softly as she opened it, and she jumped at the sound. She poked her head out cautiously, then glanced from side to side. Flashlight in one hand, sack in the other, she tiptoed down the hallway toward Ivan's office. Her ears were finely tuned for any footsteps or unusual noise. At each doorway in the system of tunnels she listened for activity. There was none. Kelle could feel her heart pounding as she neared Ivan's office. A sliver of yellow light shone from beneath his door.

Kelle rapped lightly on the door.

"Come in."

Taking one last glance over her shoulder, she entered the director's office. Ivan immediately rose to his feet.

"What's happened?" he demanded. "You're white as a ghost."

Kelle mustered up a weak smile and dropped the plastic bag on his cluttered desk. "Someone wiggled my doorknob and left this as a calling card."

"Sit down," Ivan instructed as he sank back into his desk chair.

"There's a printed message in there somewhere." Sitting on the edge of her chair, she watched him filter through the burnt ashes.

"Burn with me," she quoted as though it had indeed been burned into her mind.

Ivan found the scrap of paper and twisted it around so he could read the message for himself. His hand raked through his thinning gray hair. Displeasure and distaste were clearly etched in his pale blue eyes as they read and reread the message. With the edge of one hand he scraped the ashes back into the bag.

Tightlipped, he asked, "Did anybody hang around you today?"

Should she voice her suspicions? she wondered. Should she tell him about Ensign Taylor? Or Schwartz? Or . . . no, she told herself. She didn't want to damage anyone's reputation with wild accusations.

"No, sir," she answered. "Nothing out of the ordinary happened."

Kelle knew her speech was rushed and her voice sounded breathless, but she couldn't help it. She was too upset and nervous to speak normally.

"We'll have to take precautions to make certain this doesn't happen again," he murmured. "You aren't going to like this, Kelle, but you are about to become my shadow. I could trust your care to Mike, or Carroll, but I think it would be best if I took over now. There isn't a man here who would dare do anything while you're with the director of the program. Smacks too much of mutiny."

"But what about my work? I can't expect you to hang around the infirmary while I'm conducting my research."

"Your safety is the primary concern."

Kelle couldn't argue with the wisdom of his decision. "I don't like it, but I guess I don't have any choice, do I?"

Shaking his head, Ivan stood up. "I'll shut down early tonight." He opened the center drawer of his desk and slid the bag into it. "Let me get some order into this confusing mess on my desk and we'll retire for the night. The room next to mine is vacant and it has a communicating door. You'll be safe there."

Ivan began sorting through the piles of papers on his desk, putting them back in their proper folders. Leaning back in the chair, Kelle relaxed for the first time since she'd heard the footsteps outside her door. As though her memory dredged up the sound, she heard someone rapidly coming down the corridor. Instantly sitting up, her body twisted toward the entrance of the room.

Panic must have shown in her eyes. Swiftly Ivan moved around the desk and placed his hand on her shoulder. They both heard the sharp rap. The door swung open.

"Sorry to bother you, sir," the radio communications officer, Jason Sullivan, said, "but I just received a medical emergency communication from Mc Murdo. Carroll Kleinschmidt's youngest son has been hospitalized. He's in critical condition."

Kelle felt her breath catch in her throat. Not Carroll's son, she silently protested. She'd heard so much about the boy she felt as though she knew Billy herself. "Any details?"

"Not at this time. Mc Murdo wants to know if there is any possibility of landing a helicopter here. Over on the coast the weather seems to be clearing out enough to risk a flight," Jason concluded.

"Escort Dr. Langdon to Kleinschmidt's room," Ivan instructed, briskly taking command. Ivan grasped Kelle's forearm. "I'll check out the weather. If the wind currents have died down we'll try to get him out of here."

Minutes later Kelle, breathless, stood outside the room in which Carroll and three other men slept.

"Jason, you go in and get him. Don't tell him anything other than the doctor wants to see him as quickly as possible. I'll wait out here."

The young navy officer slipped quietly into the room. Kelle paced outside the door. Any thoughts of personal danger disappeared under the more pressing concern for her friend. As a doctor, she was used to being the bearer of bad news, but she never found it easy. This time, however, it would be especially difficult and there wasn't any way to soften the blow.

Her back was to the door when it opened. Spinning around, she looped her arm through Carroll's and headed down the corridor before speaking. "We've had radio contact with Mc Murdo. Billy is very ill. He's in critical condition in the hospital."

Out of the corner of her eye she watched the color fade from Carroll's face. "I thought you were in trouble. Oh, my God . . . not Billy!" His voice was anguished and his steps faltered. "My wife will be destroyed if something happens to one of the kids. Is she okay? She'll be worried sick. Can that affect her pregnancy?" He spoke rapidly, searching her face for some reassurance.

"Your wife must have initiated the radio communication. She's strong, Carroll. She'll cope. You know she will," Kelle reassured. "Nothing has happened to her or we'd know about it. Ivan is checking out the possibility of getting you out of here right away. Mc Murdo Station thinks the weather has cleared up enough to risk a flight over here."

Carroll squeezed her hand, silently thanking her for the comforting words. "Jason, what do you think the chances are for getting out of here?"

"Can't say, sir. The last storm seems to have diminished in force, but, at best, the weather is unpredictable."

One by one they filed into the cramped radio room. The sound of static came over the radio operator's set.

"Anything new?" Carroll demanded, laying his hand on the operator's shoulder to get his attention.

"I expect contact in"—he glanced at his watch—"five, maybe ten minutes. Sooner if anything has happened."

Kelle looked at Carroll's ashen face. "Are you all right?" she asked. She had suspected for quite a while that Carroll's physical condition was not what it should be. He was older than most of the members of the team and Kelle had thought he exhibited some signs of an incipient heart condition. She knew the dangers of shock and was becoming increasingly worried about his condition. "You're not having any chest pains, are you?"

"I'm fine," he responded curtly. "Damn it, I should be there. What the hell am I doing at the South Pole when my child is dying?"

"We don't know that he's dying, Carroll. You couldn't have prevented your child from becoming ill," she reasoned softly. "Don't blame yourself."

With a nod toward Jason and the doorway,

she gave Carroll's shoulders a final squeeze and stepped outside the small room. "I'm going to my office to get some tranquilizers for Carroll. Tell Dr. Svensky where I've gone."

The next few hours would be nervewracking for Carroll. Kelle couldn't do anything to relieve his anxiety over his son, but she could prescribe medication to calm him down.

Quickly she moved down the corridor away from the radio room. Everyone must be asleep, she thought, observing the lack of any kind of activity.

Suddenly she heard a sound behind her. Kelle listened intently. Not now, she begged silently. Quickening her pace, fear making her heart thud loudly in her chest, she wished she had the nerve to call out, but she didn't. Whoever followed her seemed to be running also. Rounding the corner, Kelle rushed into her office and hastily shut the door behind herself.

Ear pressed against the door, panting softly, she waited. Nothing. Maybe my imagination is working overtime, she thought, shoulders slumping.

"Leave the light off," a raspy voice wheezed. "We'll make a fire of our own."

Danger wasn't outside the door . . . it was in there, waiting for her. Kelle fought the overwhelming desire to scream, to let the darkness in the room surround her mind and blot out the devastating fear inside her. Mind barely ruling emotion, she flipped the light switch upward. A blaze of light cut through the frightening darkness.

Frank Carson, the cook's assistant, leaned back in the chair behind her desk. The light momentarily blinded him. His arm raised to protect his eyes, but Kelle could see the leer on his face.

"I've been waiting here a long time for you, Doc. I've got the same disease as Mike Johnson, and I want some of your special treatments."

"Get up and get out of here right now, Carson," Kelle answered once she swallowed the lump of fear in her throat. He's a coward, she reminded herself. He's afraid of open exposure. "You so much as put one finger on me and I'll scream loud enough to be heard in New Zealand. How do you feel about spending the next several years in prison? There aren't any women there either."

A frightened shrill laugh seemed to burp from between his lips. "Nobody's gonna tell. We'll all—"

"Carson, I'm going to count to three and you'd better be moving toward the door. Carroll needs my help, and I'm not going to waste my time here with you."

Her tone jarred Carson into an upright position. Taking advantage of his obvious dilemma,

Kelle forced herself to walk steadily and confidently toward the medicine cabinet.

"One," she said ominously.

"Now wait a minute. You can't buffalo me into—"

"Two . . ."

"No woman is going to threaten me," he blustered. Nervously he laughed and made a tentative move toward her.

Kelle reached for the small suture scissors in the cabinet, determined to do whatever she had to to thwart him.

They both spun toward the door as it was suddenly thrown open.

"Kelle . . . you okay?" Mike growled, instantly aware of the tension in the small office. "Carson. What are you doing here? You sick?"

Knees trembling from relief, from fear and shock, Kelle propped herself up against the examining table. "Carson's sick all right. And he thinks I'm the cure."

"I didn't touch her. She's the crazy one. Lured me in here. Said she wanted—" Carson whined pathetically.

"Shut your foul mouth, Carson, before I shut it for you." Mike took several steps toward the smaller man. His fists clenched at his side.

"Mike! That's enough." Stepping between the giant whose face flushed with rage and the coward cringing behind the desk, Kelle grabbed Mike's arm. "Stop it. I think Carroll needs medical attention."

"So does Frank Carson," Mike ground out between tightly clenched teeth. "Nobody is going to spread filthy lies about you while I'm around."

"Not lies," Frank squeaked. "She's slept with half the men here!"

Mike lunged across the desk, grabbing Frank by the shirt front. Off-balance, he still managed to lift Carson off the floor, shake him violently, and fling him like a rag doll back into the chair. "One word, mister. One more filthy word and I'll be around this desk pounding your face."

"Stop it. Damn it!" Kelle clenched her hands into the woolen fabric of Mike's shirt and tugged with no visible effect.

He turned, grabbing her upper arms, and demanded, "What were you doing running around through the halls?"

"I came in here to get tranquilizers for Carroll." Not wasting words, she gave a brief account of the radio message delivered while she was in the director's office.

Legs wobbly, she hesitated long enough to recover her equilibrium, then went to the medicine cabinet. She opened the glass door and extracted the necessary pills. "I have to get back over there."

"You're not going anywhere unless I'm

along," Mike asserted. "Get up, Carson. You're going, too. We'll let Svensky decide what to do with you."

Wordlessly Carson rose to his feet and shuffled toward the door. Head bent, he didn't look at Kelle.

In single file, Carson, Mike, then Kelle wended their way back to the radio room. Mike grabbed Carson by the shoulder none too gently to allow Kelle to enter the room without having to brush by him.

"Any news?" she asked while she opened the bottle of pills and shook two out into the palm of her hand.

"Ivan thinks I might be out of here in six hours or less," Carroll replied. "What are those?"

"Valium. They won't knock you out, but they will calm you down. Do you need water?"

"I'll take them dry." Carroll gave his hand a sharp shake before holding it out to receive the pills.

Out of the corner of her eye, Kelle saw Ivan move past the doorway. Then she heard Mike's low voice explaining what had happened. Seconds later Ivan entered the room.

"One problem sorted out," he whispered softly as he passed by. He crooked his finger in her direction and pointed toward the hallway. Once they were outside the room, alone, he stated, "I've decided to send you out with Carroll. Carson may not be the only hostile man. I'll have Mike pack up your personal belongings. Besides, I'm worried about Carroll. I need you to keep an eye on him should there be a change in the report on his son. Okay?"

For a moment she wanted to argue that anyone could go with Carroll, but she realized that Ivan was right. Carroll might need medical care. But she hated the idea of leaving the Pole before the expedition ended. Bailing out before her work was completed distressed her.

Nodding her head in agreement, she set personal ambition aside. Pitted against the health and welfare of her friend, it ran a poor second. Carroll might need her both as a friend and as a physician.

Ivan patted her shoulder in condolence, then strode back into the radio room. "Carroll, it's looking good. But you know it's risky. If our luck holds you'll be on a plane headed toward New Zealand within hours. Unless there are personal items you specifically need, I'll ask Mike to have Schwartz pack your belongings."

"I need to talk to Petersen before I go."

Kelle marveled at the man's emotional control. Although obviously desperately worried about what was taking place in a hospital in New Orleans, he still had the capacity to temporarily set worry aside and tie up a few loose scientific ends.

"When you've wrapped up your business I want to go through the emergency survival procedures with you. Getting you out of the Antarctic is going to be tricky. Why don't you and Kelle go into the lounge and I'll send Petersen in there."

Carroll began to shake his head, unwilling to leave the communications room.

"Jason will bring any news," Ivan said.

"Come on, Carroll. You're better off in the lounge. I'll buy you a cup of coffee," Kelle offered.

The lines of strain and tension momentarily disappeared from his face. With effort he forced a smile in Ivan's direction and quipped, "If you find a cup of dimes after we leave, they're Kelle's. She can't adjust to the idea of free coffee."

Ivan chuckled, then gave Carroll a comradely slap on the shoulder. "We'll have you out of here on your way home as quickly as possible."

As promised, Kelle poured the coffee once Carroll had settled himself into the armchair at the table.

"What do you think Billy has?" Carroll asked when she set the cup in front of him.

"Could be anything. He's always been

healthy, I know you've said. That's in his favor. Kids are resilient. I've seen them come into the hospital in critical condition and three days later be laughing with their parents in their room." Kelle responded with soothing confidence while silently praying Billy's case would work out that way.

"He's a tough kid." Using the heels of both hands he rubbed his eyes. "I never thought anything like this could happen. They worried about something happening to me."

"Are the pills taking effect? They may make you slightly drowsy."

Lowering his hands, he rested them on the white surface of the table. "I'll be okay."

"I'm going to check your pulse rate," Kelle informed him as she reached across the table and picked up his wrist. High normal, she thought as she felt the pulse beneath her fingertips and silently counted. "It's in the high range, but that's to be expected. Every four hours I want you to take two more pills."

"Sorry to hear about your family emergency," Petersen said as he strode into the room with a roll of papers under his arm. "Can we give these a onceover?"

Kelle stood and moved away as the two men pored over the sheets. She had added an extra spoonful of sugar to her own coffee to counteract the shock her own system had undergone.

The sweet flavor made the brew difficult for her to swallow. Her mind couldn't move away from thinking of what might have happened if she hadn't been able to control Carson.

Carson. She would never have suspected him. But it made sense, now that she thought about it. He must have been the person who removed the food tray from the infirmary. In the days she'd had the trays delivered, whoever brought them never opened the door wider than necessary. Had Carson inadvertently pushed the door open wide enough to see her in bed with Mike?

Schwartz had headed her list of suspects. Glancing at the dart board, she wondered how the rumor had been spread. From the assistant cook, to the head cook, to special friends as they picked up their food? Anything was possible.

Ensign Taylor probably had added fuel to the fire by tossing in his tidbit of gossip regarding the friendly hug she'd given Carroll. She was sure he'd done his best to make her appear promiscuous.

Silently, sadly, Kelle sighed. Her role in the polar expedition was unexpectedly drawing to a premature end. Instead of having time to neatly wind up the strings, she was leaving uncompleted work behind her. And would she ever see Mike Johnson again? Would he seek her out? Or would he consider their brief affair as a highlight of his adventure at the Pole and nothing more?

While Kelle thought, Mike was emptying her clothing drawers. There was something decidedly intimate about touching the silky undergarments a woman wore. He tried to handle them as though they were the woolen shirts he had removed from the bottom drawer, but he couldn't. They reminded him of the soft satin texture of her skin. A sachet in the back of the drawer explained their spring-wildflower fragrance.

You're acting like a melancholy fool, he admonished, picking up the bundle of lacy scraps and carefully adding them to her suitcase. He'd already packed up everything she had in the bathroom. Glancing around the room, it saddened him to see all trace of Dr. Kelle Langdon packed neatly away into one large suitcase and one small cosmetics case.

Taking a notepad out of his shirt pocket, he carefully copied down the name and address off the identification sticker on the cases. He might or might not have a chance to speak to her alone. He wasn't taking any chances on losing track of her. Once the expedition had been wrapped up, he had every intention of heading toward Texas.

## CHAPTER SEVEN

Sunlight awakened Kelle. Its late-fall brightness filtered through the bedroom drapes, making shadowed patterns on her pale-blue coverlet. She could feel the warmth on her forearm and lightly trailed her fingers over the blond hairs. It's such a contrast, she thought, to the dark, sunless world of the South Pole. Content to lie in the early-morning sun, she mentally retraced her frantic steps between the Pole and Houston.

Personal survival equipment stowed under her seat in the helicopter, Kelle had climbed in, nervously anticipating their hasty departure. The harrowing flight from the Scott-Amundsen base to Mc Murdo, followed by a flight to New Zealand, then another to New

Orleans, had been exhausting. Then after making sure that Carroll's son was all right she had made the final dragging steps up to her Clear Lake condo.

Kelle stretched. She had promised herself two full days of sleep when she'd finally eased her travel-weary bones into bed, but when she put on her glasses and glanced at the digital readout on her calendar clock, she was surprised to see she'd slept less than twelve hours.

Nothing has changed, she thought, examining the room bathed in the pure light that streamed through the ceiling-to-floor windows. Only me.

In the long hours of transcontinental flight she had contemplated those changes over and over in her mind. She had felt displaced by the abrupt departure. There hadn't been time for a farewell party, a gentle breaking off of relationships with the promise of a reunion in the future. She regretted being unable to have a few moments of conversation with Mike. They were both very private people by nature, and they hadn't been able to ignore the men standing around them and make any kind of plans for the future.

Mike had shaken her hand along with the others and muttered, "See you."

*See you.* Kelle had heard similar departure lines from other men. Seldom was the casual promise kept. No amount of hoping, praying, or sitting by the telephone could make it ring. Mike could get her address from Ivan, but would he?

Sitting up, Kelle hooked her arms over her legs. Perhaps her hasty departure would save her embarrassment and heartache in the long run. There were no vows of undying love shared, no promises of where and when they would get together. Just a simple handshake. Kelle closed her eyes and visualized Mike the way she'd seen him once she had climbed into the helicopter.

Dressed in his red parka, hood drawn over his head leaving only the darkness of his face visible, thick wool pants windblown against his muscular thighs, mukluks on his feet, he resembled the other men who were standing beside him. His height made him distinguishable from the others, but only until the helicopter had lifted. The red bundles waved until Kelle could no longer see them in the darkness.

"Perhaps being unable to distinguish him from the others is prophetic," she murmured. "Will he disappear from sight forever as the others did?"

Kelle swung her legs off the bed and stood up. Melancholy doesn't suit you, she admonished. Her life had not begun at the South Pole, and it wouldn't end now that she was no longer there. Silently she admitted to meeting and falling in love with a wonderful, sensitive man, but hadn't she prepared herself for disappointment from the beginning? She knew that, when given an option, the Mike Johnsons of the world would only be interested in beautiful women. He had been attracted to her only because she had been the only woman available. She knew she would have to do her best to put him out of her mind forever.

"And if you're smart you'll start now," she told herself firmly.

Her jaw thrust forward at the challenge. There were reports to write for the National Science Foundation in Washington. There were grant proposals to write. And, most important, she needed to contact Rick Gibson at the space center. Long before the spacelab was actually built, members of the teams that would man it would be chosen. She wanted her name at the top of the list.

"One doesn't sit around waiting for something to happen," she reminded herself. "One *makes* it happen."

Kelle chuckled. Her old habit of talking to herself hadn't taken long to resurface. There were other habits she'd enjoy also. Walking into her huge beige bathroom, she eyed the shower stall and anticipated something she'd missed terribly at the Pole—a long, hot shower with no concern about wasting water. In Texas there weren't any ice melters to stoke. She could lather, rinse, and lather again if it pleased her. And it did. When she left the bathroom squeaky clean from the crown of her head to the tip of her toes, she blessed the Houston water company.

Deciding on her course of action, she picked up the telephone, dialed the space center number, and settled in a chair next to the window. The two-story condo overlooked the salty waters of Clear Lake. While she waited to be connected with Rick Gibson, her eyes followed a single sailboat lazily circling on the far side of the lake.

"Rick? Kelle Langdon."

"Kelle? Is this long distance from the Pole?"

"Sure. And it's collect," Kelle teased, mentally picturing the short, spare man she was talking to. "How about lunch at Frenchie's?"

"They have the best Italian food in Texas, but they don't deliver to the South Pole." Rick laughed. "And the trip is a bit far for me to make during lunch hour so forget carry-outs."

Kelle laughed. "It's good to be home just to listen to you. Can you get away for lunch?"

"Sure, if you can tell me the reason for your unscheduled return."

"Nothing top secret. One of the scientist's children was hospitalized and listed in critical condition. His pregnant wife complicated the problem. We had a temporary break in the weather. So . . . here I am."

"How's the wife and child?"

"His wife held up as well as could be expected, but her husband being on the way helped. The boy is out of danger. His illness was easier to treat than what happened at the Pole."

"Now you have my curiosity up. How about Frenchie's at say . . . noon?"

"My mouth is watering. See you then."

A few hours later, Kelle walked into Frenchie's. The strong smell of garlic reminded her of the joke she and Mike had shared. There weren't any polar bears in Clear Lake City either. The pictures on the bulletin board of the famous and not-so-famous patrons, the quick hug from the part owner, Frankie, then an enthusiastic hug from Rick made her spirits soar. It was good to be home. The three of them laughed and joked as Frankie led them to a special table reserved for old favorite customers.

"The usual?" Frankie asked. He poured two goblets of Italian red wine.

"Terrific. Nobody makes fettucini Alfredo the way you do," Kelle responded, meaning every word.

"My little polar penguin. . . . It's good to

have you back!" Frankie pinched her cheek, almost knocking her glasses off.

Her thoughts returned to another man removing her glasses. A man with brown-rimmed blue eyes. Eyes that pierced her heart.

"You're a bit pale, but otherwise you look great," Rick complimented as he sat down across from her. "You are back, aren't you?" Rick quizzed with a laugh.

Glasses restored to the bridge of her nose, Kelle nodded. "We have a definite lack of sunshine at the Pole at this time of year," she reminded him with a smile.

"Was it exciting?"

"Yes. It's a long way from a nine-to-five job."

"God, yes. It's probably a hell of a lot more fun than being at the space center studying moon rocks like I'm doing. What's on your agenda?"

"Scientists don't waste much time on social amenities, do they?" Kelle teased.

"Not with you. But speaking of swapping ice stories . . . where's your Three Hundred Club button? Surely you qualified for the club."

"Believe it or not, I didn't. Immodesty wasn't enough to keep me warm."

Rick laughed. "Sometimes I almost forget you're a woman." When he realized what he had said he blushed. "Must be due to your being a foot taller than I am."

"Keep up the smooth talk, Rick, and I won't ask any favors from you," Kelle replied, grinning at her friend's discomfort. They'd been friends for a long time. Too long for her to be offended by the truth.

"Name your favor. It's yours," Rick glibly promised in return.

"By hook or crook, I'd like to be considered for the spacelab mission."

Rick stopped eating his salad. "I can't fulfill your every wish, you know. Care to ask for something else?"

"Nope."

"You couldn't be the first woman at the Pole, so you want to be one of the first women in space?"

"Nope. In fact, I hope there will be several other women along, but . . ." Kelle paused, trying to formulate a reason for her burning desire. "Remember when we graduated from the University of Texas and you asked me, jokingly, what I wanted to be when I grew up? Do you remember my answer?"

"Some wisecrack about growing up to be tall enough to reach the stars. I thought you were kidding about being the tallest girl in the class. Do you mean back then you wanted to be a part of the space program?"

Kelle nodded.

"Nothing like long-range goals," Rick said dryly. "We both know you're more than qualified for the spacelab, but there's a lot of politics behind the project."

"Such as?"

"Who you know. How well you're known. Funding. Prior experience." Rick shrugged, indicating the list could lengthen.

"Well, let's see. I know you, for starters. My experience wintering over at the Pole should be in my favor. My medical record is immaculate." Kelle watched him nod in agreement. She laughed and added, "I can train my ears to be pointed and you can call me Ms. Spock if it would help."

"Speaking of ears . . ." Rick chuckled. "I may have an ear with the higher-ups but that's all."

"Modesty suits you, but I know better. If I have you pleading my case, they'll do more than listen."

"Have you thought about preparing the path for me?" Rick quizzed. He pushed his salad bowl to the side of the table and leaned forward. "We need public support for the space program. The public backing a project means more funding."

"What do you want me to do? Stand on the corner of El Camino and Bay Area Boulevard with 'Send this girl to the spacelab camp' printed on my shirt?"

"No," Rick answered thoughtfully. "But your jaunt to the Pole could be worth some good publicity. I have some contacts with the Houston *Post* and the Houston *Chronicle*. A human-interest story, perhaps? Lone woman at the Pole type information. How you felt isolated with nineteen men. The public will love it!"

"Just a minute, Rick. I don't like the idea of cheap publicity." Kelle shoved her salad aside. "You've got to come up with something better than that."

Frankie, seeing they had both finished their salads, brought their main course over. Even the delightful aroma of her favorite dish couldn't bring a smile to Kelle's face. Rick's expression told her he was thinking about other ways in which he might be able to publicize her return.

"The news media—television, radio—they'd be interested. I could line up a list of public speaking engagements too. Remember the news coverage the woman astronaut received? I'm certain her name is on the 'most likely' list for the spacelab."

"Whoa. Back up three paces and watch my mouth." Exaggerating the lip movement, she whispered, "No."

"Come on, Kelle. It's a good idea. I know you're publicity shy, but look at Michael Jackson."

"Michael Jackson? The rock singer? For chrissake, does he want to perform at the spacelab?" Kelle jeered.

Rick burst into laughter. "He is extremely shy, but it didn't stop him from breaking the record for Grammy awards, did it?"

"You want me to hide behind reflective sunglasses? I'd rather stand on the street corner with a cup."

"Most people would give anything for the press coverage you can get," Rick retorted. "And I like the sunglass idea. Sort of gimmickie. People could speculate about snowblindness."

"That's dumb! More likely people would wonder what drugs I was taking." Kelle laughed.

"Does that mean you'll consider trying for a little publicity?" A gleam of triumph shone in his dark eyes.

Kelle squirmed inwardly when she thought about people finding out about the secondary reason for her early departure from the Pole. Would that just lead to another spate of innuendoes? She chewed at the side of her cheek. But would they ever find out? Chances were the only thing they could report would be unclassified information she revealed.

Silently she nodded her head. To begin the mild deception, she adroitly changed the topic of conversation.

"How do you manage to talk me into these things? Remember the time you talked me into standing guard at the women's dorm while you and your buddies raided the laundry room?"

"But it all worked out, didn't it? I repented immediately, and three years later married the girl whose clothes I stole."

Kelle saw his brown eyes twinkling outrageously. "That's not how you met Martha. She'd smash your moon rocks if she heard you tell those lies."

A smug smile on his face, Rick asked, "How do you know that isn't how I met her?"

Twirling the fettucine on her fork, she stared at him with mock seriousness. "You wouldn't lie to me, would you?"

"Not about anything important," he answered, neither admitting nor denying the wild tale. "Incidentally, don't wear your glasses."

"What do you suggest I use to see with?"

"Fake it. Don't you know when you take them off that myopic vision of yours makes you peer at people as though they are whispering highly classified military secrets? Besides, your glasses reflect flashbulbs. Too bad you don't have time to get contacts."

Ever so slowly, Kelle slid the glasses down her nose. Immediately his face blurred. "For your information, Mr. Gibson, I already own a set."

"So why don't you wear them?"

His voice sounded puzzled; Kelle couldn't distinguish the features on his face.

"They're a bother. Glasses are easier." Kelle shrugged.

"But you *will* wear them for interviews, won't you?"

"You are really pushing hard, my friend." She used her forefinger to slide her glasses back in place.

With fettucine dangling from his fork he replied offhandedly, "Every girl needs a mother at some point in her life. Now, about your hair. I think down would—"

"Mother Rick?" she scoffed.

Ignoring her words, Rick continued, "Maybe a permanent . . . lots of curls running down your back."

"I think you've gone too far. I can get along fine without you reconstructing me from head to toe. My clothes were next on your makeover list, weren't they?"

"I wouldn't tell you if I didn't love you like a sister."

"Love me a little less, okay? I'll do what has to be done to get the job, but I'm not going to blow my savings on designer clothes, or hair cuts, or . . . a fat-ladies' farm."

"You're not fat. Did I say you were fat?" His tone seemed completely aggrieved by her allegation, but his eyes sparkled with humor. "I'll start the media ball rolling this afternoon. Now, tell me about your latest adventure."

Kelle wasn't certain she relished the change of topic. How could she tell her perceptive friend about wintering over at the Pole without having him pick up on her personal involvement with a teammate? The mood he was in right now, he'd think passion in the frigid interior of the Antarctica would be great for press releases!

Being careful not to mention Mike Johnson, she told Rick about the theories tested by the scientists during the dark polar winter. Within minutes Rick switched from the role of mischievous friend to serious scientist. By the time they had finished their blueberry-topped cheesecake, Rick had given her ideas as to what would appeal to the public and how to present them.

When Kelle entered her condo, she had mixed emotions about the luncheon. Rick, gregarious, outgoing, well loved by all, couldn't comprehend her reticence. Even though they had been friends for years, he didn't realize that the openness they shared was restricted to a one-on-one relationship. Kelle could cope with one or even a few people without any problem, but the thought of speaking to a group numbering more than five petrified her.

Crossing to the bathroom, she rummaged through the bottom drawer of the vanity table searching for her contact lenses. They've probably shriveled up and died by now, she thought, certain her fate would be to follow the same path. Shoved in the back of the drawer she found the sealed white case and all the equipment necessary to take care of the lenses. Kelle twisted the lid labeled *L* and, much to her surprise, found the lens moist. If she planned on wearing them for any length of time, she knew she would have to begin by wearing them for short intervals.

"Now or never," she muttered, setting the case on the marble top and washing her hands.

## CHAPTER EIGHT

"Never?" Kelle asked, hiding a secret smile.

The young reporter returned a smug smile. "No. I *never* twist the facts or editorialize to make a story sensational. And even if I did, I wouldn't have to in your case."

"You can drop me off in the side parking lot if you would, please," she answered, still skeptical of his words. "I appreciate the interview and the lift home."

"My pleasure. Call me and let me know how you like the article." The newspaperman stopped the car. "I have time to come in for a drink," he suggested blatantly, his eyes appreciatively resting on her fair, Nordic features that were accented by the pale-blue suit she wore.

Laughing, Kelle opened the door. "I haven't restocked my liquor cabinet. How about a raincheck?"

The smug smile faded. "Coffee?"

"I've been so busy the past two weeks I haven't been to the store. I'm like *old* Mother Hubbard. The cabinets are bare," Kelle said, attempting to gently point out the difference in their ages.

"I like older women," he replied quickly. "They know who they are, where they've been, and where they're going. Age is in the eye of the beholder. And to me, you look ageless."

Chuckling, Kelle opened the door and got out. "Thanks again for the ride."

With a merry, lighthearted wave, she started down the sidewalk toward the lake. The media had been exceptionally kind during the past ten days. Kind enough to dub Dr. Kelle Langdon the Most Eligible Spacelab Candidate. Despite her shyness, Kelle was thrilled at the attention she was receiving.

She glanced toward the lake and saw a giant-sized man, dressed in navy slacks and a short-sleeved white shirt, standing alone on the dock. When he turned and she saw his profile, she gasped at his remarkable resemblance to Mike Johnson. This man didn't have a beard

. . . just a bushy moustache. His dark hair, neatly shorn, feathered in the lake breeze.

As she stared at him, Kelle's eyes widened in disbelief and her heart began to beat faster and harder. Could it really be? she wondered. All this time she hadn't allowed herself to believe Mike would follow her, but it must be him. She could never mistake that face.

"Mike?" she asked, her voice unsteady.

A wide, beguiling smile parted his lips as he turned toward her.

"Mike?" she called louder.

"Dr. Langdon, I presume?"

Joyfully Kelle ran, stopping only when she was wrapped in his strong arms. Mike lifted her off her feet and lightly swung her around and around, both of them laughing like children.

"I almost didn't recognize you," she whispered when her toes were back on the ground. Laughing, she blurted out her next thought. "God, you're handsome."

A throaty chuckle and a hard swift kiss thanked Kelle for her honest compliment. "You make me feel ten feet tall."

"You've always been that tall!"

"Hmm." Mike nipped the sensitive curve of her neck. "You smell like sunshine and salt water."

Kelle leaned back and traced the side of her

forefinger down his closely shaven cheek. "Missing something, aren't you?"

"The only thing I was missing was you." He lightly fingered her crown of braids. "Care to show me the insides of this castle on the lake? Or do you plan on standing on the balcony and letting down your braids for me to climb?"

"Ouch! Romantic idea, but I think we should use the conventional manner."

Pressing another quick kiss on her upturned lips, he turned her toward the condo. "It seems like an eternity since I've held you."

"I'd just about given up hope," Kelle admitted. She slid her hand up the hard muscles covering his back.

"You knew I'd come."

"Did I?" Kelle planted a soft kiss beside his slightly turned up moustache.

"I'll give you an hour to stop that," Mike warned with a low chuckle.

Distracted by his presence, Kelle fumbled in her shoulder bag searching for the key while her bright-blue eyes stared at his face. Without his beard and shaggy hair, Mike Johnson was every woman's dream man. Her newfound confidence, inflated by the press coverage, began to wane. Why is such a handsome man on my doorstep? she couldn't help but wonder.

As though he heard her question, Mike lowered his head, nibbled her ear, and whispered,

"I love you, Dr. Kelle Langdon. More than I thought I'd ever love any woman."

"I love you too," she answered. Totally forgetting about the key, Kelle raised her parted lips.

Her experience was limited, but she knew when his lips slowly lowered and met hers, this would be love's sweetest kiss.

The forgotten purse slid off her shoulder. She raised on tiptoe and circled his shoulders as he gently wound his arms around her waist and lifted her higher. Both slightly trembling, they melted against each other. Mike separated her lips further with the tip of his tongue. Her waist against his, her arms fully around his shoulders, his hands fanned over her hips as he cradled her closer to his rising need. Impatient, frustrated by lonely weeks of dreams, hours of waiting, he thrust his tongue into the honeyed interior of her mouth. The low groan he heard was like a lit match flaring against dry kindling. He pressed her lower body closer as he tasted her sweetness.

"Kelle, love, take me inside. Love me."

Those were the words she'd dreamed of hearing. Her heart—or was it his?—beat loudly in her ear. "The key is in my purse."

Mike retrieved the purse, opened it, and took out the key. As though he entered her apartment regularly, he picked out the apartment key and unlocked the door. Wordlessly she took his hand and led him up the carpeted steps to her bedroom. Standing beside the bed, eyes feasting on each other, they quickly shed their clothing. Their need was great. Too great for pretense or delay.

The moist, achy feeling Kelle had suppressed for weeks flowed through her body. Once in bed, Mike clamped her against his body, swiftly entering her. Sheathed completely in her soft womanhood, he groaned as though he'd been waiting all his life to be a part of her.

Kelle sucked a deep gulp of air into her lungs when he thrust powerfully. The desire to cling to him brought her legs up to wrap around his waist. She held him deep within, relishing the exploding sensations as each rhythmical jolt increased her own ecstasy. Her hips arching to meet his, she gave as well as took. Fiery passion quickly erupted, hurling both of them over the precipice into a star-studded heaven of their own making.

Mike collapsed to the side of Kelle. He cradled her in his arms. Their breath came in gasps as though they had starved their lungs while gorging their passionate needs.

"That wasn't the way I intended on loving you," Mike said in a low voice. "I had wanted to make up for being rough the first time."

Her arm around his waist, Kelle roamed her hand over his heated, damp back. "Rough?" She peppered the dark hair on his chest with sharp kisses. "Apologize and I'll shove you off the bed. Dreams are powder puffs next to the real thing."

"Did you dream about me?"

"Mmm-hum. Day dreams. Night dreams. And most of the time in between."

"Me too." With one hand he began taking her hairpins out. "Making love to Dr. Langdon, hair bound tightly around your head, was wonderful. But I'd like to cuddle with Kelle. Hey, that sounds like a pop tune, doesn't it? 'Cuddle with Kelle.' "

She lifted her head to give him access to the pins on the right side of her head. Amusement and fulfillment and love lit her pale-blue eyes as she ran a fingertip over his arched eyebrow. His brown-rimmed, sky-blue eyes echoed her sentiments. Once he had her hair loose, he playfully swished the ends across her buttocks. Kelle laughed and pressed a hard kiss on his waiting lips, the soft moustache scratching and tickling her mouth.

"If 'Cuddle with Kelle' is on one side of the record, what's on the flip side?" she teased lightly when his hands seemed unable to choose between threading through her hair and stroking the tips of her breasts.

" 'Love Me Again'?" he whispered as his lips lowered and solved his dilemma. Gently he teased her nipple with his tongue, then sucked its fullness into the hot, moist interior.

Kelle murmured, "Yes, my diamond in the rough. Love me. Love me."

As he pressed a kiss into the valley between her breasts before nuzzling and capturing the other budding tip between his lips, Kelle draped her leg over his hip and drew him closer. She wanted to feel the unleashed virility of his manhood. Once was not enough for either of them.

The edge of his passion slightly dulled, Mike made love to her the way he had in his dreams. Slowly his hands explored each sensitive zone he'd thought of during the cold, lonely nights he had spent at the South Pole. The tantalizing warmth of her body drove him time and time again close to taking her, but he didn't. He teased and stimulated until Kelle, no longer able to stand the sweet torment, rolled him on his back and straddled him.

"You're driving me crazy," she groaned hoarsely. "Two can play that game."

For each erogenous area he had tantalized, she found a corresponding place on his muscular body. She fondled his chest with her hands as she lightly massaged his manhood with the downy soft hair of her femininity. She quickly learned the exultation of provoking him to mindless wonder. The agony of pleasure was clearly expressed on his face as he restrained from grabbing her hips, positioning her, and driving upward forcefully.

"I'll beg if you want me to," he ground out between his clenched jaws. "Do you want to hear me beg?"

"Tell me," Kelle encouraged, bending down to catch every passionate word.

And he did. Words he had never used, sweet words, passionate words, loving words, told her precisely how much he wanted her, how much he loved her, how desirable she was. And she told him how much he added to her life, how she had longed to have him with her, how she had become a passionate woman under his tutelage. When words were no longer enough, Mike raised his hips and silently awaited her. His eyes, directly below hers, glowed with love and anticipation. Ever so slowly Kelle claimed him until he was completely hers . . . as she was his.

Afterward, a deep satiated calm claimed them both. Both would have slept for hours, but the sound of the telephone jarred them awake. Reaching over him, Kelle picked up the receiver.

"Hello."

Because she was so close Mike could hear

both sides of the conversation. Her voice immediately took on a businesslike briskness. Why was the Houston *Post* requesting an interview? Television? A half-hour program with three other spacelab candidates? Reception at a country club? His hand aimlessly slid back and forth over her hair down to her rounded bare skin. A chill crept up his backbone as Kelle hung the phone up.

"What was that all about?" he asked, sitting up.

"Just a little public relations work. I'm trying to get my name to the top of the roster for the spacelab expedition." Kelle swung her legs off the bed and reached for her robe. She slipped it on before turning around and facing Mike. "How about some dinner?"

"The spacelab isn't even built yet. Isn't this a bit premature?"

"Not really. The teams are chosen and trained over a year in advance."

"And you're planning to be one of them?"

"You knew that. Remember? I told you about my ambition down at the Pole." Kelle grinned at the dismay evident on his face. "They'll need mechanical engineers up there too."

"True, but the number applying will be far greater than the number of physicians applying—especially those with your qualifications."

"Maybe I can pull some strings," Kelle teased.

Mike grunted, disdainfully replying, "The only strings I want you to pull for me are the ones tying your robe shut."

Smile drooping, Kelle wondered what was wrong with Mike. Dissatisfaction could be clearly seen on his face.

Mike glanced at the window. "Where did the sunshine disappear to?"

"It's seven thirty, Mike. Come on downstairs. The best I can offer is a sandwich. Is that okay?"

Mike managed a forced smile. Nodding in silent agreement, he climbed out of the bed. Once Kelle had left the room he noticed a pile of clippings and photographs collected on the bedroom desk.

The slacks he had discarded earlier lay crumpled in a heap beside his feet. He crossed the room to the adjoining bathroom and cleaned up before getting dressed and rifling through the pages of newspaper and magazine articles. Pride in Kelle partially restored his good humor, but the fear of losing her increased. The clippings pointed out the differences between them. The chances of his being included in the spacelab mission were negligible. Kelle would make it and he'd be left behind, just as he had when she'd left the Pole.

Maybe their differences were too much. Maybe love wasn't enough. He didn't doubt her love, but how could he be sure he'd be able to keep it? The hushed comments he had overheard after Kelle had left the South Pole had weakened his confidence. Some of the men had found it very amusing that the doctor had chosen the diesel mechanic? The mocking voices had hurt him deeply. The newspapers would have a blast if they got hold of the story, he thought sadly. Was love about to make a public fool out of him?

"No!" he said vehemently.

He realized their love, the love he wanted to make into a permanent relationship, didn't stand a chance. If he loved her—truly, unselfishly loved Kelle—he would have to be content with what she could give him. Maybe a week, maybe a month, maybe if he was lucky, a year, but he wouldn't be a millstone around her neck keeping her earthbound.

I'll know when the time comes to leave, he silently promised himself. Oh, God, give me the strength to let go when the time comes.

Kelle pulled the outside leaves off a head of lettuce and placed them one by one on boiled ham. Everything had been wonderful up until that damned phone call, she thought. Could it be Mike resented the newspaper calling? She spread mayonnaise on one side of the bread.

She had been kidding about pulling strings for him. But surely if publicity could tilt the odds in her favor, maybe it could also help him. With a nod of her head, she knew convincing Mike to become a part of her little media blitz wouldn't be easy. But perhaps I can convince him it's fun, she thought, trying to find an easy solution to their problem.

When Mike entered the kitchen, Kelle had just finished making the sandwiches. "Sit down. What do you want to drink?"

"Do you have a beer?"

"I think so." Kelle opened the refrigerator and racked her brain for a way to introduce the subject of publicity.

"I saw the articles upstairs on your desk. You've been a busy lady."

Kelle smiled. Great minds run on the same channel, she thought. "An old friend of mine, Rick Gibson, suggested getting some coverage. Who ever thought plain Kelle Langdon's face would be in the newspapers?" She gave Mike his beer, picked up the plate holding his sandwich, and crossed to the dinette table. "I have several interviews lined up. Care to join me?"

"I'll be happy to go along and listen," Mike answered, trying to dodge the question without being blunt.

"No. I meant join me in the interviews. These articles have generated a curiosity about the polar expedition." Kelle moved back to the kitchen counter and picked up her sandwich and milk.

"I'm a private person, Kelle. Besides, your being there was unique, but my role was relatively unimportant."

"Don't be modest. What would have happened if the equipment had broken down? Disaster!" she argued.

"There isn't any glamour or mystique about fixing engines. Generally people view doctors as miniature gods." Mike held up his hand to stop her from interrupting. "What works to get you at the top of the roster wouldn't work for me."

"But, Mike, it's fun!" Her enthusiasm sounded hollow to her own ears. She knew she didn't sound convincing.

"For you, I'm certain it is. For me? It would be sheer hell. Thanks, but no thanks. The sandwich is delicious." Mike smiled, trying to change the topic. "You do any fishing from the dock?"

"Not much. Will you just go with me on one interview?"

"How about crab nets? When I was in Florida years ago, we chased them through the surf with something that resembled butterfly nets."

"Crab traps. How about the interview?" she persisted tenaciously.

"No. Crab traps? That's cheating. The crab doesn't have a chance. How about chicken wings tied to a string? Have you ever tried that?"

"Mike . . . damn it!"

"Kelle . . . damn it!" he echoed, laughing. "I know you're mad when you start cursing. Now listen, love, and listen carefully. I won't stop you from doing whatever you have to do to reach your goals, but don't push me in the same direction. Okay? I've got some plans of my own," he lied. "But first I want to take a few weeks off and rest and spend as much time as possible with my favorite member of the medical profession.

"I'll keep busy. Don't worry about me. If I get bored I might do something really crazy—get a job."

"Where did you originally plan to go after returning from the expedition?"

"Someplace warm." Mike laughed jovially. "I have a standing job offer in Wyoming, but I think I'll wait until the snow stops flying to accept it."

"A standing job offer? Doing what?"

"A relative is the operating engineer of a mine in Wyoming. My family lives in Cheyenne and they're constantly trying to get me back home."

"That's a long way from Houston," Kelle

commented. Her spirits took a plunge downward. Was Houston just a stopover on his way to Wyoming? She raised her eyes hoping for an answer.

Mike reached over and held her chin between his thumb and forefinger. "I'll be here awhile, if that's what you want."

"You know I do," she whispered sincerely.

"Then there is nothing for you to worry your pretty little head about. I'll never leave as long as you want me here. Which brings me to another topic. My luggage is at the Holiday Inn. Are those the closest living accommodations?"

"There is someplace much closer. How about my room?" she offered with a smile.

Mike nodded and began eating enthusiastically. "I thought you'd never ask," he answered, beaming.

"I want you to stay with me as long as you want to," Kelle said sincerely. "Want to walk along the waterfront after we eat? Texans are a friendly bunch. Maybe one of them will offer to take you fishing."

"A romantic walk with my woman *minus* the friendly Texans is more to my liking. I can meet the locals while you're out gallivanting."

It was evident to Kelle that Mike wouldn't allow her to arrange anything for him. They were incredibly close in some ways, but in others they were still miles apart. Would they ever be able to accept help from each other the way people in love should? Or would something always stand between them?

## CHAPTER NINE

Mike grinned when he saw Kelle getting out of the used LeBaron she'd recently bought. She had been like a kid shopping for a new toy when they had gone from car lot to car lot in search of just the right car. She had originally protested against the idea of buying a convertible. They didn't match her conservative image. But all her resistance disappeared the moment she laid eyes on the sporty white car.

"Hey," Kelle called from the parking lot. "Did the lotus eater catch anything for dinner or is it canned tuna . . . again?"

Pulling up a crab trap filled with clawing live crabs, Mike shouted, "Get the water boiling, lady. You're in for a feast tonight."

The skirt of her pink cotton shirtwaist billowed in the wind as she walked toward the pier. "You cheated! What happened to the chicken-wing-on-a-string routine?" she teased.

"You aren't the only one sick of tuna." Mike released the trap and it splashed back into the salty lake. "How about a kiss for your favorite fisherman?"

Kelle stretched up and lightly pecked his cheek. "I could get used to this."

"If you're going to get used to something, try this," Mike growled, pulling her into a close embrace.

He kissed her with the same fervor they had shared since he had come to Houston three weeks ago. Kelle swayed against him, letting him feel the quick hardening of her nipples.

"I'll remember that one," she promised, her voice low and throaty. "How was your day?"

"Slow . . . but getting better moment by moment," Mike answered as he playfully swatted her rear. "How was yours?"

Kelle groaned. "I've heard politicians gripe about the creamed chicken circuit and laughed, but I can empathize now. Don't catering services know about beef and pork?"

"Good thing your favorite chef knows your preferences, huh?" The meaningful look he gave her told Kelle he was privy to all her preferences.

"Late dinner again tonight?"

"Nope. We're going to settle into a normal workday routine."

"We aren't going to get a little physical exercise to work up an appetite?" Kelle laughed and poked Mike in the ribs. "Why change a delightful routine?"

Taking her hand Mike kissed her fingertips. "I got a job."

"A job? Why? Doing what?"

"One question at a time." Mike swung their arms together as he led Kelle up the walk. "Why? Because three weeks of loafing around is enough. I can't let you support me in the manner I'd like to be accustomed to. Hurts my manly pride." He was half teasing but half serious. "And doing what? Practicing my trade, of course. It's nothing permanent. Part-time job as a mechanic for the boat company down the road."

"Why boat engines? You could get a job at NASA, the space center, by snapping your fingers."

Mike held the door open and allowed Kelle to precede him into the condo. The odor of the seafood casserole he had put in the oven permeated the room. Walking into the kitchen, he picked up a hot pad, opened the oven door, and removed their dinner.

"It's only part time. Enough to pay for my share of the food and still give me time to cook it," he answered with a chuckle. "Your hours are irregular so a nine-to-five job for me is impractical."

"But, Mike," she protested automatically, "you're wasting your ability."

"Get the plates and silverware, would you?" he asked, slipping the hot pad under the dish and placing the casserole on the table. "It isn't a career move, Kelle." He shrugged as he watched her arm raise to lift the plates. The sweet upward thrust of her breasts made him wish he was putting the casserole in the oven instead of taking it out. "Three weeks of vacationing has been fun, but I'm starting to get dishpan hands."

"You don't have to do dishes," Kelle responded defensively. As she set the plates on the table she saw the ends of his dark moustache twitching. "Keep your hands out of the dishwasher while it's in operation, you big tease!"

With a boyish smile on his face, he leaned back and retorted, "It was get a job, man, or listen to my lady nag."

"Nag! I do *not* nag!"

"What do you call your not-so-subtle hints about sharing my experiences at the Pole with the press? Don't deny it."

Mouth open, Kelle stopped her insincere denial. "Okay. I admit to *gently persuading* you to join me, but . . ." Kelle watched his eyebrow arch higher. "But I don't want you to get bored and search for . . . excitement."

"Excitement being synonymous with woman-hunting?"

Kelle openly shared the fear she'd kept tucked away. "There are a multitude of Texas beauties who would love to be escorted around by you while I'm not around."

Mike burst out laughing. "You discovered my secret fitness program. Daily I beat them off with my fishing pole." He flexed his biceps to illustrate the success of his muscle-building program.

Drawing away, upset by having him laugh at her private doubts, Kelle sat down in her chair. "You probably do," she muttered.

"I have not even looked at another woman since I came to Houston." Mike couldn't keep from chuckling as he picked up her clenched fist. "Kelle," he whispered coaxingly, "I love you. Trust me."

"I'm sorry." She raised her eyes from the reflection on the dinner plate. "Maybe I haven't figured out why you love me."

"Are you crying? Or are those damned contacts bothering you?"

"Both," Kelle answered, sniffing delicately.

"Go take them out. Why you can't wear your glasses beats me."

Kelle knocked her chair over in her haste to flee up the stairs. Tears threatened to wash her contacts out of her eyes. He doesn't understand, she lamented tearfully. She heard Mike pounding up the stairs after her.

"Kelle . . . ?"

"Go away," she shouted as she ran into the bathroom and locked the door.

The flat of his hand smacked the door as he shouted, "Kelle! Damn it, Kelle. I thought you were kidding around. Every television station, every newspaper, every God damned man, woman, and child in this part of Texas has heard about Dr. Kelle Langdon by now. Haven't you read the articles?" Mike stormed over to the desk, grabbed the latest clippings and began reading: " 'Dr. Kelle Langdon, beautiful, blond, and brainy!' How about this one?" he roared, tossing the first one into the air. " 'Kelle Langdon returns to Houston and reveals the problems of isolation at the South Pole. The attractive blonde compared life at the Pole with future spacelabs.' Do I need to read more? You're a celebrity and you can't understand why I love you?"

"That's hype! Publicity!"

"Hype? Every day I wonder how long you're going to allow me to stay in your exalted presence!"

Kelle flung the bathroom door open, banging it against the tile wall. "You don't mean that."

"Mean what? That you're the local star? That you're living with someone who isn't qualified to wipe your shoes? That—"

Kelle stopped the flow of words by cupping her palm over his mouth. "I'm not a star, a celebrity, or anything like that. All that stuff in the paper doesn't mean anything. And I want you here. I love you, Mike. Maybe I'll never understand why you're here, why you stay, but I love you."

Fiercely Mike crushed Kelle against him, as if by holding her tightly he could absorb her, make her a part of him forever. "Oh, lady, I'm scared to death you'll wake up some morning, take one look at me, and tell me to kiss off."

"I'll never ask you to leave." To convince him she spread kisses over his cheeks and jaw line.

Mike reached under her knees, lifted her off the floor, and carried her to the bed.

Face buried into her neck, he told her over and over again how he loved her. But he still couldn't believe she really wanted him. He choked back his own doubts in an effort to calm Kelle.

Kelle rocked against his hard body. Nothing she could say could convince him that what the media said was unimportant. Why had she lied initially and told him the press coverage and interviews were fun? Why had she constantly pushed him in the direction she was taking? With only the best of intentions in mind, she had hurt him and as a result had hurt herself.

Tears streamed down her cheeks unchecked. Deep sobs shook her shoulders. Even though she had removed her contacts, her eyes felt as though grains of sand were glued to the underside of her eyelids.

"Kelle, don't cry. Please don't cry," Mike pleaded. "I'm sorry I blew up. You're so precious to me. It tears my guts out to see you cry like this." In atonement Mike wiped away the moisture with his fingertips, then his lips.

"I'm sorry too. I shouldn't have run away from the table. But your laughing made me so damned mad. Those articles don't mean a thing. They took a Plain Jane and—"

"Shhh, love. You aren't plain. Not to me and not to anyone else. Please stop crying."

A shudder and a hiccup ended her tears. When she looked into Mike's eyes, she saw the misery she had caused. With soothing strokes she crossed her thumbs over his brow. How could she doubt him? Almost at the same instant, she thought, How can you not doubt him? He's the answer to all your dreams rolled into one. He's just too good to be true.

The telephone rang. Mike rolled over and

picked up the receiver. "Hello." He paused, listening to Rick Gibson rave about the appearances Kelle had been making. Unseen by Kelle, Mike rolled his eyes toward the ceiling. "It's for you. I'll go down and fix a salad."

He handed Kelle the phone and strode out of the room. Dr. Kelle Langdon's public wanted her. That was more important than clearing up any misunderstandings! In the kitchen Mike removed a head of lettuce, carrots, celery, and a cucumber from the refrigerator and began assembling a salad.

I'm like a God damn housekeeper, he silently gritted, with stud service thrown in on the side for good measure. He ripped apart mercilessly the tender leaves of lettuce. He knew he was wallowing in self-pity, but damn it, he hurt. Why hadn't she been tickled that he had obtained temporary employment? How long did she think he could sit on his hands waiting for her to bless him with her company?

Mike scraped the carrot then sliced it along with the celery and cucumber into the glass bowl filled with lettuce. He had been half joking about dishpan hands, but there was an element of truth to his teasing.

Damn it! Her crocodile tears really did a job on me. I'm the one who should be bawling my eyes out!

The switch in feminine and masculine roles

had been sticking in his craw for the past week. Didn't she realize that's why he had found employment? Did she want a tame little puppy dog happily trailing along after her? I'm supposed to wag my tail in ecstasy each time she pats me on the head. I'm supposed to lap up any attention she manages to throw my way. Hell, I even fetch the paper off the front steps!

He was working himself up for a fight and he knew it. The status quo isn't acceptable, he thought. I won't start another round of tears, but things are going to change . . . tomorrow.

Kelle hung the phone up and stared at her feet miserably. She realized Mike had been restless the past few days, but she hadn't thought much about it. Hadn't he enjoyed relaxing in the sun? Sure, she had been busy, but he always knew where she was going and what she was doing. She couldn't say the same for him. Mike could have been conducting a flaming affair with any number of women and she would have been left completely in the dark. But she hadn't thrown a temper tantrum about how he spent his time.

All her publicity events were beginning to wear her tolerance down. Didn't he comprehend that just having him in the audience would make these functions more tolerable? Even Rick had mentioned Mike's lack of enthusiasm whenever a reporter appeared. On the rare occasions when he did happen to be along, Mike managed to disappear until the very end. How could he resent something he adamantly refused to be a part of?

"And now he has a job," Kelle muttered as though she was alone. "What kind of job does he get? A temporary job! One he can walk away from. Doesn't that tell you anything, Kelle, old girl?"

You bet it does, she answered silently. He found a job with no responsibilities . . . no commitments, no future, because he doesn't plan on sticking around long. Oh, yes, he *says* he loves you. But isn't that what most men say? He even admitted he didn't want to return to Wyoming while the snow is flying. A nice little intimate stopover in Houston suited his needs perfectly. Momentarily she hoped the Rocky Mountains would have blizzard after blizzard during the long winter months.

Mike had made it perfectly clear he wasn't going to allow her to influence his life. She could nag, moan, groan, and bitch, but it wouldn't change his plans. He lived here now. Settle for now, she advised herself. The here and now was better to think about than the bleak future.

When Kelle came down the stairs, she joined Mike in the kitchen and began mixing the salad dressing. Mike watched. Vinegar, water, seasoning, and oil were poured into a small jar. Once the lid was on, Kelle shook it vigorously. The oil didn't mix with the other ingredients. Again she shook it, harder. Mike took it from her hands and energetically agitated the mixture. Finally it began to blend.

"I have a feeling we're like the salad dressing . . ." Mike huffed as he gave the jar a robust shaking, determined to end the separation.

Kelle smiled at his diligence. "But nothing tastes better, does it?"

"No . . . it's worth the extra trouble." He poured the dressing over the salad and tossed in some croutons. Their love was worth the trouble too, he agreed silently.

Throughout dinner they were polite, cautious about what they said. They sat close to each other watching television, but a silent barrier kept them apart. Finally, after the local news, Mike stretched and said, "I'm going to bed. Tomorrow is a work day."

"I'm giving a lecture at the Clear Lake Division of the University of Houston. Afterward the professors are taking me out to dinner. Want to join us?"

"No thanks, just bring a doggy bag home." The edge of the cutting reply was smoothed by a wide smile. "Dr. Langdon, you are cordially invited to share your bed." *Just don't ask me to sleep at the foot,* he added silently.

Kelle gracefully rose to her feet. "Want to take a quick stroll?"

"Not tonight. Fighting takes it out of me."

"Can I get you something?"

"No. I'll go on to bed and sleep it off."

Minutes later, they lay side by side without touching. It wasn't the first night they had gone to bed without making love, but it was the first night neither of them said "I love you."

Mike controlled his breathing to keep it steady. Arms folded behind his head, he tried to figure out what he could do to bridge the wide crevasse between them. She hated the thought of his puttering around with diesel engines. And he had to admit to being jealous of her success. If another man infringed on his territory he would have known what to do: grab him by the scruff of the neck and kick him right out of her life. But a printing press and a camera? Where do you kick them? How do you fight inanimate objects? Kelle loved being the darling of the media more than she loved him; that's what it all boiled down to.

The first rays of sunlight coming in the window awakened Mike. He still felt angry and hurt, but he regretted the way he'd acted the night before.

He turned his head on the pillow and stared at her. She's lovely, he thought, memorizing each feature. To me she's beautiful inside and out.

"Kelle? Wake up, love," he said with a huskiness in his tone.

"I'm going to sleep in," she protested sleepily.

Mike propped his head up on one hand. "I have to go to work."

Snuggling close, draping her arm limply around his waist, Kelle shook her head. She felt the hairs on his chest tickling her nose. "You're going to be late."

Chuckling aloud as she pulled herself into the cradle his pelvic bones made, he knew she was right. He wouldn't apologize again for his behavior; he'd show her how much he loved her. With great tenderness he caressed her awake and made love to her. Each stroke, each kiss, each thrust was a silent avowal of his love. And it was beautiful . . . just as she was.

## CHAPTER TEN

Kelle ate breakfast alone for the first time in a month. She missed having Mike across the table reading snatches of newspaper articles that interested both of them. Earlier when she had started to get out of bed, Mike had firmly pressed her shoulders back against the pillows and told her to sleep late. Had she remembered how awful it was to eat by herself, she would have insisted on getting up. But she had felt so quiet and peaceful after their lovemaking that she had drifted into a light sleep.

The stack of notes for her report to the National Science Foundation had been neglected for too long. She needed to compile the information on various tests she had conducted at the Pole while her mind was fresh and Mike wasn't around to distract her. Three hours of uninterrupted work should get them organized, she thought. She leaned back and drained the last sip of coffee from her cup.

"I'll fix Mike some Texas chili for dinner," she murmured aloud.

She regretted that she had accepted a dinner invitation, but at the time, she had thought she could convince Mike to join them. How wrong I was to think I could manipulate him, she thought with a grimace. He isn't about to be led around by apron strings. Kelle giggled, remembering his dishpan-hands complaint. His getting a part-time job as a boat mechanic didn't utilize his capabilities, but if dabbling around with engines kept him content, who was she to object? Mike would always be his own man charting his own course.

Kelle shrugged as she walked to the counter and poured herself another cup of coffee, then picked up her notes off the bookcase and headed to the sliding door leading to the patio. A light breeze rustled the pages and blew strands of hair across her face. She breathed in deeply as she contemplated the work ahead of her. Within minutes she became completely absorbed in her report.

The sun drifted toward the west side of the building before she realized how swiftly the hours had passed. She restacked the work with a feeling of accomplishment. At last she was ready to start the actual writing. When she glanced at the clock over the fireplace as she slid the patio door open, she realized she would have to rush to throw together Mike's chili and get dressed for the speaking engagement.

Later as Mike jogged down NASA Boulevard toward the apartment, he wondered why he was running instead of walking. Kelle wouldn't be home until late. His pace slowed as he turned into the condo complex. For once her coming in dog-tired didn't matter. He had spent the day working on repairing the diesel engine in a shrimp boat. His jeans and T-shirt were filthy. Oil had splattered down his arms and his hands were grimy. And yet, he felt good. Kelle was busy; he was busy.

As he walked by the building next to Kelle's, a neighbor recognized him and waved. Mike returned the greeting and started to strike up a conversation until he saw the distasteful look on the man's face as he examined Mike's grease-covered clothes. What the hell, he thought, unwilling to let the white-collar business exec deflate his self-esteem. Honest work, whether clean or dirty, wasn't to be sneered at.

Mike ran his palms down the stitching of his jeans. Oily fingerprints on the door weren't appealing to anyone. He unlocked the door and opened it.

"Chili," he murmured aloud, identifying the odor in the apartment. It pleased him to know Kelle had fixed something for his dinner.

Whistling, he strode into the kitchen and got a beer out of the refrigerator. The sound of the front door opening startled him.

"Kelle! What a pleasant surprise." He set the beer down and welcomed her with open arms.

Her first instinct was to fling herself into his arms the way she normally did until she noticed that he was covered with grease and oil.

"I had a half an hour so I thought I'd stop by on my way to the Hilton." She avoided stepping into his arms. "Don't get me greasy. I don't have time to change clothes."

Mike recoiled as though he had been slapped. He felt like a fool with his arms extended and Kelle backing away from him. Worse than that, for the first time he felt dirty.

"I'm glad you found time in your busy schedule to drop by," he lied, wishing she hadn't bothered.

"Is that sarcasm I hear? Would you rather I hadn't?"

Disappointed over his lack of enthusiasm, she tossed her purse on the sofa and entered the small kitchen.

"What's the point if I can't even give you a hello kiss?" His blue eyes glared at her.

"Do you want me to arrive at the dinner with handprints on my clothes and grime on my face?"

"Soil the illustrious doctor with my filth? Heaven forbid!"

"Mike, I don't have time to rehash the argument we finished this morning."

"Just dropped by long enough to pick up the paper? Well, lady, you're going to have to cut your own clippings. Pardon me while I go shower." With careful deliberation he maneuvered himself out of the room, making a point of not getting anywhere near her.

Her own temper flaring, Kelle strode back into the living room and picked up her purse. "Don't be a jerk," she muttered.

Mike came to a dead halt on the steps. In a quietly controlled voice he said, "Good-bye, Dr. Langdon. I'd kiss you, but I can't. Have a good dinner."

Slamming the door behind herself, Kelle fumed as she ran toward her car. Some appreciation he had shown for her making an extra effort to see him! It wasn't her fault he hadn't had time to clean up. She regretted calling him a jerk, but damn it, did he think she wanted oil all over her clothes? And those snide remarks about the newspaper had hit home with the impact of a sledgehammer. She'd explained about the hype. Hadn't he noticed she was no longer front-page news? As she had expected, the press coverage was drying up to a mere trickle. Besides, whose idea was it to put the clippings into a scrapbook? Not hers. He was the one who had stopped her from pitching them in the wastebasket when she cleaned up the bedroom.

Once inside the car, Kelle twisted the key with a vengeance and revved up the motor. Mike had overreacted to everything she said. She hadn't come home spoiling for a fight, but she wasn't about to back down. Let him think about it. By the time I get home he'll realize how ridiculous he sounded, she thought.

Mike felt far from ridiculous. He scrubbed his skin until every trace of grime had been removed, then he lathered up his hair and washed it. The time had come. Their arguing two days in a row told him he had outstayed his welcome. He'd known from the beginning their love had burned too intensely. But he thought he'd be wise enough to exit graciously before being thrown out.

"How egotistical," he muttered.

He turned the shower off. Kelle calling me a jerk is the final piece of the puzzle, he thought. He knew it for sure now. The doctor and the mechanic weren't compatible. The kindest thing he could do would be to walk out and never look back.

A lump formed in his throat and seemed to grow larger. He knew he was making the right decision, to pack and leave before she returned from dinner. "But, oh God." He groaned. "It hurts. How can I live without her?"

Kelle opened the front door. During the entire meal she had fought the urge to pick up her purse and hurry back to the apartment. Once she had had a chance to cool off, she realized the worst choice she could have made was to leave Mike. She should have stayed and tried to work things through. By the end of the week all the publicity work would be over. Then, if necessary, she would ask him to consider legitimizing their relationship. She needed that formal piece of paper, a marriage license, to eradicate her insecurities.

The fear she'd fought all evening suddenly overwhelmed her. He was gone.

"Mike?"

The interior of the condo was absolutely quiet. The lingering smell of burned chili hung in the air. She flipped on the light and rushed into the kitchen. Maybe he's gone out to get something, she hoped fervently, clutching at any straw. The kitchen had been cleaned immaculately. A note was taped to the refrigerator door.

Hand trembling, she snatched it down. She squeezed her eyes shut to blink back the moisture gathering in the corners.

"My lady," she read, gulping loudly. "Grab a handful of stars for me. Love, Mike."

Kelle bit her lip to keep her teeth from chattering. The bold script on the paper wavered in front of her. Neatly she folded the small sheet of paper. Mike was gone; she didn't know where.

With heavy footsteps she climbed the stairs, forgetting everything in her usual nightly routine. The light left on in the kitchen didn't matter; it couldn't shed any light into the dark void in her life. The door remained unlocked. Why lock it? She had lost the most valuable thing in her life. What remained for anyone to steal?

The phone began ringing when she crawled into bed still clothed. Kelle pulled the covers over her head to muffle the noise. The only person she wanted to talk to was Mike Johnson. And he wouldn't call. He'd never call. Never ever again.

Opening her eyes when the jangling stopped, Kelle remembered another time when she had huddled under the covers and felt as though life wasn't worth living. She had been nine. Skinny, gawky, ugly Kelle Langdon had been chosen by a wonderful older couple. They wanted to adopt her, to make her part of their family, their home. Elated at the prospect, she had made every effort to be "a good little girl." Kelle remembered eating every morsel of food put on her plate, scrubbing her body until it was squeaky clean, helping her foster mother with any chores. And then, even though she had been so very, very good . . . the bottom had dropped out of her young world. She wasn't available for adoption. The nice couple cried; she cried; her foster parents cried. The State of Texas had decreed that she live in limbo.

And here, years and years later, she felt as if she were again living in limbo. How odd, she thought. As a child a legal document had stopped her from having a home with someone to love her. And now, as an adult, she would never have the legal document that would make her belong to Mike.

Kelle lowered the covers. A kid can't do anything about it, but you're an adult! she told herself. Flinging the covers back, Kelle turned on the light, unfolded the note in her hand, and read it again. "Lady" and "Love" glared out at her.

"Mike is hurting too!" she exclaimed. "He isn't walking out because he doesn't love me

. . . he's walking out because he *does* love me."

Where is he? she asked silently. Where would he go? Where would I go if I felt hurt?

"Home! I'd go home to people who loved me," she babbled excitedly as she reached for the phone. "Wyoming. He's headed for Wyoming."

She called one of the largest airlines at Hobby Airport, and after what seemed like forever a voice answered, saying, "May I help you?"

Kelle stood up. "Yes. Yes, you can . . . if you will. I need to have someone paged. His name is Mike Johnson. He may not be flying this airline, but . . . oh, please, could you page him anyway?"

"Certainly. Please hold."

Ear pressed to the phone, she could hear the paging system calling his name. "Come on, Mike. Be there. Be there."

She paced in an arc around the nightstand. Again she heard his name being paged. A few minutes later her silent prayers were answered.

"Hello," a familiar low voice responded.

"Mike? Mike Johnson, don't you dare fly out of Houston. I love you. I don't want a handful of stars . . . I want you. Damn it, don't you know I can't live without you? You asked me once if I wanted to hear you beg and I said yes. Is that what you want from me? Oh, love, I'll drop on bended knee and beg."

"I called you a few minutes ago. I couldn't do it. I just couldn't leave you." His voice sounded choked with emotion.

"I'll be there as fast as I can. Just wait out front."

Kelle hung up the phone and dashed down the stairs two at a time while Mike thanked the woman who had called him to the phone. He hadn't gone more than ten steps toward the automatic door when he heard the same woman shout his name.

"Another call?" he questioned, spinning around.

"No, sir. But won't you need your suitcase?"

They both laughed as he strode back and retrieved his leather bag. "Guess I'm more excited about staying than I was about leaving," he explained.

Seventeen long minutes later Mike watched a sporty white LeBaron speed up the ramp. When Kelle screeched to a stop, Mike opened both doors on his side. He tossed his suitcase into the backseat and climbed into the front. Kelle had her arms around his neck, showering kisses across his face before he could close the door.

"I won't let you go. Nobody ever loved me.

I'm not going to let the only person in the world who cares about me get away. Marry me. Please. Marry me." The haphazard thoughts she'd wrestled with on the freeway spewed forth without inhibition.

Mike pulled her across his lap. "Shush, love, or you'll start bawling and you know it tears me up to see you cry. I love you, lady. I thought I had to be the world's biggest jerk when I held a plane ticket in my hand and watched the last flight wing down the runway." He softly brushed back the wisps of hair and tucked them behind her ear. "But I couldn't seem to function properly without my heart. Oh, lady, I'll marry you ten times if you'll have me."

"You aren't a jerk. I didn't mean it."

"And you aren't some publicity-seeking crazy lady either. If I stop hurling insults at you about your job, do you think you could adjust to having a husband who comes home from work with oil smeared all over his face?"

Kelle shrugged, then hugged him tighter. "What's a little grease between a husband and wife? Besides," she added with lighthearted banter, "when we're living in the spacelab—"

"Dr. Kelle Langdon speaking, I presume?"

"Well, love, I didn't want you to think I'd become all weak and submissive." She nipped a path up his neck. "I want a prewedding present?"

"Name it."

"A handful of stars."

"Lady, I can't promise—"

"The stars I see when you make love to me. Or the ones I see in the morning shining in your eyes. Those stars. Love stars."

Mike cupped her head between his palms and looked into her eyes. "For as long as we live . . . the stars are yours."